WITNESS

WITNESS

WRITTEN BY
Matthew J Fratus

ARTWORK BY
Zeal Artistry ZA

RESOURCE *Publications* · Eugene, Oregon

WITNESS

Resource Publications
An Imprint of Wipf and Stock Publishers
199 W. 8th Ave., Suite 3
Eugene, OR 97401

www.wipfandstock.com

PAPERBACK ISBN: 979-8-3852-1181-4
HARDCOVER ISBN: 979-8-3852-1182-1
EBOOK ISBN: 979-8-3852-1183-8

Dedications:

This book is dedicated to each and every person who has found *or will find* Jesus as their personal savior.

Special THANK YOU to
Don Poore & Kayla Fratus

Contents

CONTENTS

Author's Note

Jesus warned in the last days, the love of most would grow cold. As a Christian, I certainly see this happening in today's world. The Bible's ending that once seemed so hard to imagine has truly come to a sobering focus. Twenty years ago, I couldn't imagine we would see the world in such a state. Like many however, the recent events of our world have called me into a deeper faith and relationship with the Lord. In that faith, is an unshakeable belief in the word of God and a putting off of self. With almost a third of the Bible being prophetic, it's so important to be anchored to it, expectantly as we await what He tells us is to come. It saddens me that many of today's churches don't teach prophecy. The focus seems more towards prosperity, sadly. Let's talk honestly about this. I believe it's an unhealthy expectation to constantly demand prosperity in a world we're meant to say goodbye to. Is the Lord generous? Surely! He will meet your needs exceedingly! I can testify to that. But the prosperity gospel doesn't always paint the right picture. We're called to endure, as Christ endured. We're called to lean on the Lord as servants, loving Him above all others and then loving those around us to the fullness of ourselves. We're called to be good stewards of the gospel, carrying with us a commission to reach the world with it. We're called to witness. As witnesses, we're given power through the Holy Spirit. The very presence of God in our hearts, our Lord and Savior died for us to have. It's the Holy Spirit that convicts us of Revelation and the signs of the times. If, as a Christian, I am so focused on what's happening for my own good, how can I possibly be ready for the calling Jesus commissioned me for or the things that now seem imminent for my generation? The Lord says—*keep watch* but prosperity says—*keep track*. I don't believe we can do these two things. So, what does this all have to do with my first sentence about love growing cold? Because love begins with the Lord, not the world or what's in it. If love grows cold, it means the presence of the Lord by His Holy Spirit, shrinks back. A falling away causes this. And it's a falling away that will precede the Lord's appearing, as is written.

Love will grow cold. While people chase the scraps of prosperity this world promises, or while they try their best to make God in *their* image, what happens is they burn out. They know *about* Christ, but they don't know Him personally. They know the hymns, but not Him. The aim of this book is to shake them from their slumber. To call to the hearts of any unbeliever that what's written here will happen in like fashion. The characters may be different, or the timing of events may be otherwise, but I assure you the events themselves will transpire. I won't debate the timing of the Rapture. It's fruitless to argue over words and only damages the hearers. Instead, I trust what the Spirit reveals. I trust what's been given to me. My advice to any and all is simply this… before you begin, pray. Ask for wisdom. Don't be afraid of experiencing what you read here, because if the Rapture hasn't happened and you're reading this, you can still be spared of the wrath that's coming through forgiveness in Jesus Christ. However, if you're reading this post-rapture, first, let me assure you, what they say has happened to those who vanished, is a lie. Next, let me plead to you, get your hands on a Bible. Not a digital one or anything of the sort, but a paper-based book. You'll need that more than anything because everything is now going to change. And my last appeal to you is this… When the Lord said to count the cost of following Him, He was serious. The Christian life is a battleground, not a playground. The minute you pick up your cross and begin to walk with it, opposition will find you. That will never be truer than during the Tribulation. A man will rise to power. He will make war with the saints. He'll be given the authority to kill them. You cannot buy or sell without taking his mark and swearing your allegiance to him. DO NOT TAKE HIS MARK. Remember, tribulation doesn't care what we believe in and neither does the Rapture. Both will happen. All who enter either do so by choice. The choice is ours to make.

Introduction

Tribulation doesn't care what we believe. Neither does the rapture. Both will happen as ordered from God, wonderfully and terribly, beyond the heavy opinions of man. Our faith in either is irrelevant to their occurring. Our faith in Jesus Christ, however, will decide which of the two we experience. I present to you a glimpse of a world I hope to never see...

God, be with those who do.

WITNESS

MATTHEW J FRATUS

Chapter 1

AZUL STOOD ON THE sands of the bank, looking out at the sea, pondering all he had ever known. A lifetime of experiences re-played in his mind. So many victories… He watched from shore, the swirling wind stirring up the waters. Gazing towards the ho-rizon, a distant storm began to slowly emerge. "How fitting." he whispered, lifting his eyes towards the rapidly darkening clouds. Suddenly, the sound he had waited to hear; a trumpet, echoed throughout the atmosphere. In the distance, a powerful roll of continuous thunder screamed from the ends of the Earth, before converging with a massive *boom*. Lightning flashed across the sky as far as any eye could see. Then, a sudden quietness came over the sky. In the distance, Azul saw the vast sweeping darkness falling over the horizon. Standing firmly in the sand, he spread his legs far apart to brace his balance, readying himself for what was coming. He looked down towards the ground and began to lower himself down with prideful anticipation. He smiled and looked up from where his feet were planted and tauntingly said, "Where is your fury for them?". Suddenly, the ground around him shook, violent-ly. He laughed at the massive vibration, as he watched the ground continuously rise and fall all around him, like loose floorboards in an old home. As he endured the perilous vibrations, Azul looked up from the crumbling ground and then eagerly out towards the horizon, as rocky cliffs in the distance tumbled effortlessly into the ocean. Then, he heard screams echoing by way of the towns and cities behind where he stood. Eager to watch the chaos without relenting his footing, he did his best to look around, hoping to see a glimpses of the carnage firsthand, as the violent shaking continued. He turned and stared out towards the darkened vastness of the surrounding sea, to see flames erupting in the distance all along the horizon. Large explosions echoed out, almost in unison. And still, the ground continued to shake without mercy. Just then, a sudden howling sound came from the clouds. Azul watched but found the shaking of the ground becoming too hard for even him to endure. Having quickly lost confidence in his footing, Azul pridefully braced himself once more and looked up to see several large airplanes, plummeting towards the ocean. The aircrafts each struck the water and seemed to evaporate on impact before the remaining wreckage engulfed the distant waters in flames. Just below his feet, the ground suddenly tore apart revealing caverns of massive depths. He leapt into the air and effortlessly hovered above the destroyed beach he was standing on, watching as the ocean began to pour itself into a great row of newly formed cracks and caverns. "That's enough of that." He said aloud with a smile, as the ground he had tried his best to stand on, was swept away in a flash. He quickly hovered higher above the chaos and marveled at the destruction all around him, as the ground continued to shake. Waves began to pour in towards where he was hovering, and soon overtook everything beneath him. Then, after taking in all the catastrophes, he turned his gaze far out across the great ocean, scowling eagerly towards the west, his eyes fixed thousands of miles off the coast. "Where is it?" he whispered, impatiently. He watched eagerly but still there was nothing. "Where is it?" he whined, his voice elevating as his impatience grew further. Then, he became enraged. Azul looked up and then flew upwards to the base of the darkened clouds. "Is it just?", he said tauntingly, while pointing towards the west. Then suddenly, a deep and awful bellow cried out from a distance. He turned and looked excitedly as it echoed out of the direction he had been watching towards. Still hovering just below the clouds, he witnessed a cluster of massive, pounding waves pour over the world's many coastlines, as a sudden underground eruption in the west, began causing immediate flooding. Screams could be heard from throughout the world as the catastrophic set of events and their wide-reaching devastation poured out. Azul marveled at the loss of life he was seeing. Yet still, he knew the worst was to come. A second massive bellow roared, immediately drowning out the screams and pleas for help. Azul flew closer toward the bellow's direction. He watched joyfully as an ominous darkness erupted from the Earth and filled the sky, as black volcanic clouds of vapor and ash began pouring out into the atmosphere. The underwater eruptions caused waves almost instantly to turn into impenetrable walls, some towering hundreds of feet. They moved in merciless rows, one after the other, seeming intent on not allowing a single survivor. The already flooded towns were immediately engulfed by the sudden arrival of the tsunamis. In the distance, every scream that clung to their hope, was instantly made silent.

Still hovering above it all, Azul turned back towards the great bellow. The sounds of screeching metal screamed across the ocean floors, as sulfur streamed out from the rocks below, emptying itself into the waters. He watched the marine life for many miles, die instantly, as the massive amounts volcanic ash poured from the depths of the ocean floor, into their inhabited waters, consuming the water's oxygen. A black, dense smoke quickly blanketed the entire west. Azul smiled, as he hovered unscathed in the raining ashes and fire as he watched the sun quickly turn black as sackcloth. "It begins." He cried out as he hovered above the destruction that had, without warning, consumed the world. Then, a sudden white light beamed brilliantly through the dark, billowing clouds, shining its way to the east. Azul looked towards its direction to see in the distance, two bright illuminations standing on the shores, immediately deterring the winds and waters from Israel. He scoffed at the sight, and looked up towards the sky, grinning wickedly. "Let them come." he said, before disappearing into the haunting inferno that was about to change the world.

Chapter 2

THEY HUDDLED TOGETHER AS each watched in terror. "This is so awful." Maya said, her eyes welling up with tears as she watched the horrors unfolding on her television. She and her family sat helplessly, as they witnessed the footage of the massive eruption that had engulfed the country Maya had called home the last two years. "Can anyone survive something like that, Abba?" She asked. "I don't think so. Not for many, many miles at least. There's just no hope." answered her father reluctantly, as he too watched in horror. Maya sobbed and shook her head. Her mother rushed towards her and hugged her. "Oh, my love, I'm so sorry. It's awful, I know." She said trying her best to comfort her ailing daughter. "I had friends there, Ima!", Maya pleaded, clutching her mother's arms. "I know. I know" Ima whispered as she held her daughter tightly. "I thank God you weren't there though, sweetie!" she said, as was her way. Ima had always tried to find the good in things. But in this moment, her words were no comfort for Maya, who immediately pulled away from her mother. "My friends from school are probably dead and that's all you can say?" She replied. Her mother began to get upset and said, "Maya, I'm sorry. I'm not trying to be selfish, but you're our daughter! I couldn't imagine what I'd do if I ever lost you!" Maya looked away from Ima, back towards the television. "They say a bunch of people are missing as well. Like the world has been attacked or something." A voice from the other room called out, as Maya's younger brother Abi ran into the room holding his cell phone out to his family. "Look!" he exclaimed as he gave Maya his phone. "All of social media is down right now, but just before this happened, I had a feeling I should take a few screenshots of what some people were saying." He said gesturing towards his phone's pictures. Maya swiped through her fourteen-year-old brother's phone. "What am I looking at Abi?" she said with frustration, as she continued to swipe angrily through Abi's photos. Abi sneered at his sister. "My phone, stupid!" he responded sharply. "Absolam!" Ima cried out. "Your sister is suffering right now!" Abi looked up to his big sister, somberly. "I'm sorry. I got overwhelmed by it and wanted to share. I'm sorry, Maya." he said calmly. Maya shrugged his comment off, before continuing to swipe through her little brother's screenshots, before shrieking... "Oh my god!" she exclaimed, as she showed Ima and Abba the picture her brother captured. Her father jumped from the couch and took the phone. He saw Maya's friend Haley had posted on social media moments before the eruption an ominous post that read.... *My family just disappeared. HELP!* "Abi, did you get another picture of this post thing?" Abba asked as he swiped through his teenage son's photos. As he did, his eyes widened at one of the images. "Oh no, what is it?" Maya asked nervously. Abba waved Ima over to show her, first. Ima looked over his shoulder.... "What the heck is that?" she asked disgusted, as both looked up from the phone towards their son, before turning it around to reveal a picture of a bikini-clad young woman. Abi blushed and grabbed his phone. "Bigger issues, guys!" Maya screamed defiantly, as she grabbed the phone to see the screenshots. "Yea bigger issues, guys." Abi said, relieved that his pictures were no longer the focus. Maya turned and scowled at her brother's sly attempt to not be punished. "Shut up, you perv." She said. She looked again at her friend Haley's posts. "It says your feed was interrupted" Maya said as she frustratingly handed the phone back to her brother. She reached into her pocket for her phone and said, "Maybe it's just yours...". She frantically opened her social media accounts. "Oh!" she yelled in frustration. "It's all of them! They're all down." She moaned. Ima pointed to the television and quipped, "Yet we have fake news access, no problem though I see...". "Mom, this isn't time for one of you're conspiracies!" Maya snapped, as she turned the volume up on the family's television. They each looked at the TV in horror at the images. "They say it's going to impact almost the entire west." Her father said. Maya wept. "This is just… Awful. It's so awful. No warnings at all." Suddenly, the news feed was interrupted.

We bring you breaking news. It would appear, the earth was in fact, just attacked. The United Nations has confirmed this attack was not of this world. Satellites have confirmed the presence of foreign entities entering Earth's atmosphere moments before something was detonated. We go live to the footage provided from tech mogul, Darrell Denotheo, who's military satellite systems captured the following images of the large group of unidentified objects seen just before the catastrophic eruption began. A warning, these images are disturbing and are not suitable for younger viewers. The catastrophe you're about to see may take months to fully measure, as the death toll is said to be innumerable.

The screen showed the images of what seemed to be large spacecrafts abducting people randomly, without warning or notice. People were seen running and trying to hide, before being snatched away by the invading force. The images then showed a large UFO, hovering over the United States before it detonated a massive explosive over Wyoming, North America. Maya and her family gasped at the image as a reporter's voice was then heard...

We do not know the reasons for this presumed attack, but experts and world leaders across the globe suspect that this was a pre-emptive strike by an other-worldly force. Many in the United Nations suspect this unprovoked attack, could be due to mounting concerns from other neighboring planets and solar systems, regarding the current and steady warming of Earth. If Earth were to continue its rapid global carbon-driven warming, despite all efforts to prevent such occurrences, the planet and its civilization may be considered an existential danger, that exceeds even our understanding. According to one anonymous military advisor for the United Nations, he says, "We've known for some time, the dangers of global warming. We all knew that it was serious. Nobody listened. They called us conspiracy theorists. They made this tragedy because of their failure to act. The blood of the missing and the dead are explicitly on their hands, as far as we're concerned." We'll bring you more updates as they are made available. As for now, the United Nations, in alignment with many of the opposing nations outside of their influence, have agreed to activate global authority over the nations as this crisis continues to affect the rest of the globe. What we know is that our world will never be the same. The age-old question has been answered. We.... Are not alone.

Chapter 3

MAYA WOKE UP SUDDENLY. Her exhausted eyes stared up towards the darkened ceiling. She turned and glanced across the dark room, to see Ima still sleeping. She quietly got herself out of bed, grabbing her robe on her way to the kitchen, turned and very carefully, closed the door behind her. In the kitchen, she began to make breakfast for herself, her mother and Abi. She filled a stone breakfast pot with different ingredients, layering each on top of the other, and placed the dish into the oven. As it began to bake, she sat at her dining table and glanced down at the pictures her mother was looking at, the evening before. She saw the photo of her parents' wedding. "Oh, Abba, we miss you." She said, as tears filled her eyes. "Is that Shakshuka?" a voice called out from behind her. "Shhhh!" she exclaimed, pointing to the closed door. "Ima's asleep, big mouth." She said, as she wiped her tears away. Abi, already dressed, just shrugged. He made his way over to the oven and opened the door to smell what Maya prepared. "Oh, that smells good. Wait… are we out of bread again?" Abi asked. "I'm going to try and get some today. They were out again yesterday. I think it's because of this drought everywhere." Maya replied to the disappointment of her younger brother. Abi shrugged once more and sat in the seat next to her. He picked up some of the scattered pictures and began to sift through them, slowly. "Can you believe it's been three years already?" he asked Maya; his voice creaking with sadness. "I know." She replied. Both sat solemnly as they recalled the moments everything seemed to fall apart. "It seems like longer, to me."

Abi said sadly, his eyes studying the floor beneath the table. "Not to me. It seems like only yesterday He was picking me up from Natbag, before..." Maya said, before stopping as her eyes once-more welled with tears. "Before everything just... Changed." She cried out softly, before shaking her head. "It could be worse, my loves", a soft voice whispered from behind where Maya and Abi were sitting. "Good morning, Ima!" Maya said. "Morning, Ma" Abi added. Maya's mother moved around the table and kissed her children on their heads, which was her morning custom. Ima then turned towards the stove and opened it. "So much Shakshuka?" she asked Maya. Abi grinned at Ima, before looking back at Maya, saying, "She's taking some to him!" Maya scowled towards her brother. "Shut up!" she whispered in fury, as she kicked his foot under the table. "Hey, ouch!" Abi said jokingly. Ima turned to confront her daughter and put her hands on her hips and said pleadingly, "Maya, please don't go and visit that dirty hobo. You don't know anything about him!". "I know he believes in Jesus!" Abi quipped, as he then immediately stood up from the table and moved to the other side of the room, smiling. "Abi!", Maya screamed. "Maya, are you kidding me? He's one of them?" Ima asked. "It's fine, Ma. He's nice. Besides, he's not one of the crazy ones." Maya assured her mother. "They were all crazy!" her mother shrieked in response, as she stormed into the bedroom. "That's why they TOOK THEM! And that's why we have all these crazy plagues going on right now. Because of their adulterous beliefs. Curse them all!" Ima said, as she slammed the door. Abi, who had tuned out his mother's rant, took the breakfast dish out of the oven. He turned to see Maya leering at him. "I hope you choke on it, creep." She said coldly. Abi laughed. Maya got up from her seat and grabbed a dish and lid, before scooping a hearty portion of the Shakshuka out of the pan. "Whoa, why does the hobo get so much?" Abi jokingly yelled, as he tried to block his sister. Maya shoved him and said, "Because the *hobo* didn't tell Ima he was messianic!". She then sealed up the food, before turning to get dressed in the bathroom.

After getting ready, Maya made her way out of the family's small apartment, down the stairs and out to the sidewalk, with a bowl of the warm food tucked under her arm. As she walked across the street, she turned to the neighboring alley to make her way down. Maya paused and turned her head slowly back to face her apartment complex. There in the second story window, she saw Ima scowling towards her from their apartment. Maya smiled sarcastically, before making a "shewing" gesture towards her mother. But Ima wouldn't budge from her unapproving gaze. Maya turned and made her way down the alley. She looked in to see if she could see her friend. "Mash'pekh?" she called out. In the shadowy distance, she saw an old man rise to his feet. "Maya!" he exclaimed excitedly. As he entered the light of view, Maya could see the friend she referred to as "Mash Mash" come into view, his tattered clothing and long grey beard unmistakably giving him away. The old man looked to be in his early to late seventies. He was frail, yet always seemed so lively. Though he had the look of someone who had not bathed in some time, his presence was never an offense to Maya, who had begun to bring him food over the last few months. His long, ash-colored hair was frayed about chaotically, from it being unmanaged. His grey and frizzy beard looked equally unkept, as it hung nearly a foot down from the old man's chin and swayed about as he would move. Mash had long reminded Maya of the elder Rabbis her father used to pray together with. "I brought breakfast!" She said with a smile, as she held up the sealed dish. "Oh, child. You are a gift!" he exclaimed joyfully. Just then she saw in the distance, 3 others behind Mash'pekh, as they turned and walked the other way from where she had entered the ally. Maya watched curiously as what appeared to be a group of young men, turned the corner and out of her sight. "New friends?" she asked playfully as she approached Mash'pekh. Mash'pekh smiled. "I'm always making new friends!" he proclaimed joyfully, as he looked at the bowl. Maya handed it to him, to his delight. He sniffed in loudly. "Shakshuka…. Maya, with cupboards so bare?" he asked, his voice sounding sympathetic, as he knew there were severe food shortages. Maya smiled. "All of Israel is suffering, Mash Mash. Shouldn't all of God's children suffer together in kindness?" She asked confidently. Mash'pekh smiled widely and nodded. "You are as wise as you are kind, my dear." He replied as he placed the bowl under his arm. "What ails you today, child?" He asked eagerly, as both made their way over to the blanket he slept on. It was their custom to sit and talk about many things, over any meal Maya would bring him. Maya walked by her friend's side and exhaled. "Ugh. Just thinking about my Abba, a lot lately." Mash'pekh sat on the concrete and put the bowl down by his side, to listen. "Oh… Mash! You can totally eat while I talk. You must be hungry!" she exclaimed, as she sat next to him and tapped his dish. "Child, I have food to eat you do not know about." He replied with a smile. Maya giggled and quipped, "Okay, weirdo.". They both laughed together.

"So, you were saying?" Mash'pekh said, eager to hear what ailed his friend. Maya looked deep into his large, brown eyes. "I miss him." She said, as her tears once more welled. Mash'pekh nodded sorrowfully. "I did not get to meet him, but I've heard nothing but wonderful things." He replied. "Yeah. You would have liked him. He was *your* type of guy." She declared with a giggle. Mash'pekh leaned in towards Maya and asked, "Shaggy? Scruffy? A finely-dressed person of great wealth?", garnering a giggle from them both. Maya paused for a moment and thought. "No, he was a lot like you. He believed there was more to us." She said as she stared towards the wall of the alley across from where they sat. "And…. He died for it." She added, before looking down and giving way to some tears. She felt Mash'pekh's hand on her shoulder. "I'm truly sorry, Maya. I know you and your family have suffered." He whispered. "I think I would have rather he was taken in the days before like the others, instead of being killed in the incursion. So many died that week." She lamented, as she thought of the horror that had overtaken Israel just a month after the disappearing, as a massive force of insurgents from other countries, suddenly invaded Israel, seeing the world's chaos as their opportunity to plunder their resources. Though Israel's sons and daughters were able to defeat their enemies almost miraculously, the toll it had taken on the country was massive, as over twenty thousand Israeli citizens had lost their lives. Mash'pekh looked at Maya and nodded, before replying, "Many indeed died. It was a sad day for Earth and for Heaven. When Israel lost its western allies and helper, our enemies were bound to attack.". Maya nodded and wiped her tears from her cheek. Then, she smiled, before declaring, "At least we're protected now though. I cannot wait until our temple is finished and to shake his hand for all he's done for our people.". She then picked herself up from the ground and wiped off the back of her jeans. "You enjoy that food, Mash Mash." She exclaimed, patting her friends' shoulder. "Be safe my dear and may the spirit of our Lord walk with you." He replied, smiling. Maya squinted at the comment and replied playfully, "Um, yea…. Happy Tuesday to you too, Mash Mash. I'll be back tomorrow with some more goodies for you." She then turned and walked out of the ally. As she came to the street once more, she looked up to her apartment window to see Ima was still watching. Maya shrugged, before raising two sarcastic thumbs in the air. Ima shook her head at her daughter's gesture and turned from the window. Maya smiled and made her way into town.

Chapter 4

LATER THAT DAY, MAYA returned home. As she walked towards her complex's door, she turned to look down the alley where Mash'pekh stayed and saw what looked to be a large group of people, huddled together. She squinted carefully to try and see through the darkness of the alley but was unable to. She recalled seeing some young boys chastising her friend a few days ago, an event not uncommon for the increasing number of homeless in Jerusalem. Concerned for her friend's well-being, she walked across the street from her apartment and peered deeper into the alley to see what the group was doing. There, a large assembly of men were standing around Mash, being prayed over. Maya watched as Mash'pekh laid his hands on each of the young men and prayed, but the words he was saying, she couldn't understand. "What language is that?" she thought to herself, curiously. She inched closer to listen in; her head now peeking fully around the corner just a few feet from where they were standing. Suddenly, she was jolted as the men in the alley erupted together, shouting at once "Amen!". Maya jumped, startled at the exclamation. She watched as the men then slowly left Mash'pekh, with a few of them even walking past her. "Good evening." One of them said politely with a smile and a nod. Maya nodded cautiously and waded through the dispersed group to where her friend was standing. "Are you ok?" she called out to him, drawing his stare. "Maya!" he shouted, excited to see her. "Hey…" she replied, her eyes curiously still looking at each of the young men passing by her. "Did you start a boy band or something, Mash Mash?" she asked with a chuckle. Mash'pekh laughed. "These are the sons of Israel!" he declared loudly in the alley, his voice echoing out into the streets. Maya cringed as she stepped closer to him. "Oh my, I didn't know that meeting was to-night." She joked, as she saw the last man there, turn and look at her, smiling, before turning back to Mash'pekh and asking, "Anything I should tell Tevah?". Mash'pekh smiled and looked back to Maya. "Tell Tevah the numbers. And tell him I've met the best Shakshuka maker in all of Israel!" he said, as he winked towards Maya. Maya blushed at the compliment. Abi had always complained about her cooking, so a compliment was new territory for her. "No, no…. Te-vah doesn't need to know about my bad cooking. He's joking." She assured the young man. The young man laughed quietly, turned, and hugged Mash'pekh. "Thank you." he said. Mash'pekh nodded and replied, "Always, young Ashem. Always. This is where we part. But be of good cheer.". Ashem stepped back, somberly and nodded to Mash'pekh. He then turned to Maya and smiled, before leav-ing the two. "A fine young man you've chosen." Mash'pekh said aloud, watching Ashem leave. Maya looked at her friend, con-fused. "What?" she asked humorously. Mash'pekh turned to her and brushed her question aside, saying "I have your bowl!". He scurried to his blanket and took out the bowl. Maya looked and saw the bowl had been cleaned, as it gleamed in the faint lighting of the alley. "Oh, you didn't have to clean it, Mash Mash" she said warmly, appreciative of the gesture. Mash'pekh smiled, and replied "You didn't have to cook it, my dear. But goodness prevailed.". Maya smiled. Since the day they first met, she had always found a strange comfort, coming from the old man. What had begun as just a few simple courtesy greetings, had somehow turned quickly into meaningful conversations between the two. He seemed to fill an unknown void in her life as a source of honesty and humility. She was grateful for the small presence he had in her life and so, it was her honor to feed him whatever she could.

"Any adventures today for you, child?" Mash'pekh asked her, eager for her tales. "No, just work. Pretty boring." She replied, before immediately adding with excitement, "Hey, did you hear we are getting the link?". Mash'pekh stared at her, with confusion for a moment, before asking, "The link?". Maya chuckled at her disconnected friend. "Sorry, link18! Ugh, sorry. Sometimes I forget you live in an alley, Mash Mash. link18 is the device that this guy, Darrell Denotheo created. It was in trials for a few years, but when the Premier was... well, when they tried to kill him, it was link18 that brought him... or saved him or whatever. Whatever happened, it was because link18. Were you in Israel when that happened, Mash Mash? For the incursion and whatnot? "I arrived just before the Premiere was killed, yes." Mash'pekh replied, as he stared out towards the brick wall across from where he and Maya were speaking. Maya chuckled. "He didn't die, Mash Mash." Mash'pekh was quiet. Maya looked over to see her friend staring. She moved the conversation along fearing she was losing his attention, saying "Anyway, he survived the assassination because of link 18. It literally healed him! Ugh. There's nobody like him.". "And you were saying you were getting this device?" Mash asked, his attention turning from the wall to Maya. "Oh right! They're rolling it out to those of us who work for the government or are in active duty. It's being said that link18 is even going to be able to solve the whole vaccine shortage issue. It enhances the body somehow. We're going to be superheroes, I guess!" she exclaimed with a laugh as she looked up to the night sky. Mash'pekh nodded, as he too looked up. Maya paused for a moment, before turning and looking towards him. She hesitated, but then confessed, saying, "My brother told me not to get it though. He's kind of like my mom though. She thinks everything is a conspiracy, ya know? You know the type.". Mash'pekh nodded, listening intently as Maya leaned towards him, with a playful smile. "What about you, Mash Mash? Are you a fan of good old-fashioned conspiracies?" she asked jokingly. Mash'pekh laughed and replied "No, I can't say I am.". "Well, that's a relief!" Maya added with a giggle.

As the two sat together a sudden quietness came over the alley. "Maya..." Mash'pekh said softly, before adding, "Would you do me a favor?". Maya looked at Mash'pekh and nodded sincerely. "Would you pray about that device before you get it?"

he continued. Maya froze for a moment. "I... Pray? Like Prayer-prayer?" she asked reluctantly, disappointed by the request. Maya was discouraged. Though her father had been a devout reader of Torah, Maya herself had never considered herself "religious". She hadn't prayed much in her life but remembered the last day she had called out to God, was to simply ask why, at her father's funeral. Maya turned towards her friend and smiled as much as she could, before confessing "God and I aren't on the best of terms right now, Mash.". Mash'pekh smiled. "Do you not know that you're just a single prayer away from being on better terms?" he asked, sincerely. Maya paused, as she looked somberly into her friend's eyes; her mind emersed in his words. She broke suddenly, from her stare... "I am.... I.... Have. Have you eaten tonight?" she asked, desperate to change the subject. Mash chuckled at Maya's evading and said, "Child, I have food to eat you do not know about.". Maya shrugged, and replied, "Right, right, mystery food. Got it, weirdo.". She laughed playfully and turned away, toward the entrance of the alley. She paused for a moment. Out of nowhere, memories of how her father used to pray with her, began to suddenly pour into her mind. She could see herself as a little girl, proudly watching her father praying in the synagogue and at home. She marveled at the once-lost memories. As each remembrance flickered in her mind, it illuminated several other memories of her father's faith. She smiled in awe at the coincidence, as she turned back towards her friend. "Hey Mash Mash, I will pray. I promise." She assured him. He smiled and nodded. "Good, blessed night, child!" he called out. "Good night!" she replied with a smile, before turning back to her apartment complex and making her way up the stairs.

Chapter 5

As she walked up the second flight, a voice called out... "Did you see your little troublemaking friend?". Maya looked up to see Ima standing at the top of the stairway with her arms folded. "He's harmless." Maya replied, before walking past her mother. "He's not harmless, he's a heretic!" Ima shouted. "Mom, keep your voice down!" Maya said, scolding her mother. "I will not!" Ima shouted defiantly, as Maya walked into the apartment, and towards the kitchen to put the bowl Mash'pekh gave to her, in the sink. She was followed closely by her urging mother. "Do you realize they are hunting down all of these messianic street preachers before they bring another disappearing onto us?" Ima asked. Maya rolled her eyes and shrugged. "Conspiracies, Ima..." she mockingly replied. "They are not conspiracies, it's all very real!" Ima continued, before turning Maya's attention to the news. "Look! They're rounding all of them up as we speak, to avoid another disappearing! And, God-forbid, another assassination attempt on the Premier. Look! These people are going to bring another disappearing to us, just you watch!" Ima roared. Maya walked in from the kitchen and looked at the television. There she saw what her mother was describing.

The footage showed images of Christians being arrested throughout the world. Maya looked in horror. She knew the world was teetering on the belief that faith was the weakness that had brought on the disappearing, and the catastrophes that followed. She remembered those awful fears in the immediate days after, stoked throughout the world by Christians, when they boldly claimed the disappearing was what they had referred to as, "the rapture"; claims she remembered that were quickly debunked, after the world's internet was immediately replaced by WNN, the World News Network. As she watched men and women rounded up from their makeshift churches and underground prayer groups, she couldn't help but feel differently, now. The world's news displayed the graphic images of groups of people being chained together and branded, around the world, all to the applause of the reporters and analysts. The talking heads each seemed eager to brand the Christians as extremists and terrorists; world-wide threats to the quickly modernizing global society. Maya witnessed in horror as frightened Christians were being led away to unknown destinations, separated from friends and family. The correspondent who was speaking about the images, assured the viewers that these people and their beliefs was the leading danger to our world and that the United Nation's efforts to control unsanctioned worship was paramount to global peace and security. The World News Network had become increasingly emboldened, showing the graphic demise of any who were considered a threat to peace. Christian martyrdom was strewn across the television, a haunting warning to any that would continue in their unsanctioned acts of worship. "Oh my, Ima…. This isn't ok. They're really being rounded up and killed. Look at this sickness!" Maya said to her mother as she turned off the tv and turned toward her, her eyes welling with tears. Ima ran to her daughter and hugged her, saying "I know they are. I know. And I don't want to see this happen to you, dear. My God I don't. I can't lose anyone else!". Both sat down together on the couch and held each other's hands. Maya exhaled, and said as tears flowed down her cheek, "We know what this is like, Ima. The Jews know what this is like. And we know where it leads when good people stay quiet.". Ima nodded and put her head in her daughter's chest. "Oh, my sweet girl. I know we do. At times, I find myself so swept up in what that stupid television tells me, that I forget I used to refuse its every word. I don't really believe the Christians are as bad as they say, but I don't know what happened to cause the disappearing. I find myself sometimes leaning on the knowledge of the world instead of the wisdom of God, without your father around." Ima admitted, as she and Maya continued to hug each other. Both women sat silently, each doing their best to unsee what they saw. "Ya know…. Mash Mash told me that before I get link18 that I should pray about it." Maya confessed. Ima shook her head. "I caught your brother talking to that old man, too. I think even longer than you've been friends with him, Abi's been visiting him." Ima admitted to Maya's shock. Maya brushed aside Ima's comment and continued… "I remembered today Abba always prayed and asked for wisdom…". Ima smiled. "Oh, I remember. He used to wear his tassels to synagogue. He was so handsome. He was always so handsome, you're Abba." She said, warmly. Maya frowned. "Ima… we don't even celebrate Shabbat anymore." she admitted. Ima frowned. "Not since we sat shiva, I know." she said with a whimper, as she wiped away her tears. Maya melted before her mother, knowing the full weight the death of her father had on her, especially. She put her arm out to her and hugged her tightly. "I miss him too, Ima. Our world has just changed so much. Do you think Abba was right about God? Do you think he exists?" Maya asked, eager for her mother's response. Ima looked down and whimpered. "I do. I do and that's why I just don't understand any of this." She admitted. "Well, if what the Premier says happened is true, I'm sorry, but that means there is no God as we know it. If God does exist though, then we have ALL been really deceived! And if that's the case, we're gonna really need God even more. Think about it, Ima… What's happened in our world isn't clearly talked about in Torah, is it? So, either it's completely wrong and the Premier's completely right, or Torah is only the beginning of what God wanted to say to His people." Maya said, boldly. Ima shook her head. "I know Torah doesn't explain what's happening right now. I hate feeling so blind to all of this." Ima admitted. "If there *was* a book that told us what was happening, wouldn't we want to at least look at it?" Maya asked. "I suppose. God forgive us, but I suppose." She added. Suddenly, both women were startled, as a voice cried out from the doorway, behind them… "There is a book.". Abi walked in and closed the door. He walked over to the couch where his mother and sister were sitting and placed a ragged and worn Bible on the coffee table in front of the two. "Abi!" Ima yelled at the sight of the book. "No Ima..." He replied. "It's time you both listen to *me*."

Chapter 6

"WHAT ARE YOU DOING?" Danny asked Sif as he watched his friend try feverishly to straighten the pages of his old, dusty Bible. "I'm fixing it!" Sif replied sharply. "You're making it worse." Danny said, while chuckling. "Is yours any better?" Sif retorted. "Actually, it may be the only perfect one in Be'er!" Danny said proudly, lifting the book high above his head, rejoicingly. The two men then turned into an alleyway, where they were greeted by the others. "How many tonight, Tomas?" Sif asked one of the attendees. "With you two, twenty-three total!" Tomas replied. "Amen! Where are Ashem and Tevah?" Danny asked. "They are traveling up from Bethlehem. There's so much risk right now, so they waited until dark." Tomas answered before asking, "Have you all eaten?". But neither Danny nor Sif was hungry. They, like the others in attendance, knew that this night was special. They each perceived an announcement was coming from Tevah, as each stood excited about the possibility. As they were discussing it, two men emerged from the shadows of the adjacent railroad crossing. The men moved quickly across the cracked pavement, over to Tomas and the group, as both looked cautiously around the perimeter. "Greetings/!" Tomas called out to the men as they greeted them. "Tevah told us to go ahead of him and Ashem and to make sure the alley was clear!" one of the men said. "It's all clear!!" Tomas replied eagerly, as He, Danny and Sif looked down the abandoned railroad. In the distance, he could see two men emerging, slowly. It was Ashem and Tevah, walking quickly towards them. "There they are!" Sif whispered to Danny, proudly. Neither had ever seen Tevah or Ashem in person and were a bit mystified in their presence. The two well-known men made their way to the alley, to join with Tomas and the group. Ashem shook the hands of everyone there. "Brothers, it is good for us to be here!" he rejoiced. "Before we begin, has everyone eaten?" he asked the group. The group of young, eager men all nodded. Then, to the group's excitement, Tevah stepped past Ashem and made eye contact with each of the attendees. The young men stood proudly before him. He walked by each and nodded, as a colonel about to lead them into battle. He then looked back to Ashem and Tomas, with a smile and said to the group, "I believe our numbers have reached their total, as it is written. And as such, we must prepare ourselves for the next chapters of prophecy. Friends, you know who comes in a few weeks and you each know why." Each attendee's eyes fixed on the raggedy looking, elder man, who walked commandingly among them with the help of his famed, makeshift cane. "As I have shared, our time is short. We must spread the word that now is the time of haste. We will shake the foundations of human understanding and leave no heart unconfronted. You are the leaders of your groups. By the power of the Holy Spirit, we must now move as one, until it is fulfilled." Tevah said to the delight of every man there. He then walked by each man and blessed them.

He sat on the ground and had the men rest beside him. Ashem came and sat beside him. Tevah put his hand on Ashem's shoulder and said, "A great leader I leave you. Peace, I leave you. You will succeed, my friends." Ashem looked somberly at Tevah for a moment, before responding, "Amen.". Tevah turned and saw his friend had become saddened and leaned his face over to him and whispered, "You are ready for this.". Ashem nodded, reluctantly. Tevah leaned back and continued... "It must be fulfilled. You must cling to your newfound faith in Christ, our Lord. Every unsaved eye will see this. Every heart will be called through this final appeal.". Ashem put His arm around Tevah and nodded as he looked around at the group of young men surrounding them. He marveled at all he and Tevah accomplished the last few years, together. Ashem had come to learn so much from Tevah, when the two were brought together during the insurgency that happened after the disappearing. Since then, Ashem had witnessed so many great things in the older man's presence. Tevah had confided a great deal to him and the weight of what he knew was coming, was overwhelming.

Ashem leaned over to Tevah and hugged him. "I will see you soon, my friend." He said, as the two embraced. The men watching looked on, confused. Ashem then rose to his feet and called the entire group of young men together and declared aloud, "Tonight, we begin the march! Tonight, we finish our mission to go to every town and home, to proclaim His kingdom comes. We must make haste, brothers. This journey will be wrought, but it is the spirit of the Lord who goes with us.". The men nodded, with excitement. Each was eager to begin the march they were told they would be a part of. Sif looked over Ashem's shoulder, to where Tevah was still sitting. He saw that he was praying by himself, while Ashem spoke to the group. "Is he not coming with us?" He whispered to Ashem. "No, He's going to Jerusalem to be with Mash'pekh", replied Ashem. The group suddenly became nervous, as some began to wonder aloud why Tevah wasn't coming with them. Tevah finished praying, giving thanks to God for all that was achieved and all that would be. He heard the group asking Ashem questions about him and rose to his feet to speak with them. "Am I so great a man that I must go where you are called, *as well* as to where I'm called?" He asked the group in a commanding voice. The group stood suddenly silent, as none dared to respond. Tevah continued, "Whatever power you see displayed in me, is given to me by the same Father that gives you yours. It is not by me, but by Him who has called us all." He declared. The men began to nod, as their concerns began dissipating. Tevah smiled at the group, as he looked around at the brave young men, saying "You have been sealed by Him who is to come. You will be protected from the plague that comes, just as you were from the plagues that have already come. Do not be afraid. But like your brothers before you, you must go to every house, every synagogue, and every person you pass and proclaim the truth as we have shared it with you. No matter what happens from here, you each must finish your good work. You are chosen and called. This is what you must accomplish.". As Tevah said those words, he saw the men stood eager and ready for their assignment. He placed his arm on Ashem's shoulder, as each of the listeners approached them both with thanks before parting in pairs to preach throughout the nation. Ashem turned and hugged Tevah. "Thank you my friend. That was some speech." He said as they embraced. "I'm better at it than I used to be." Tevah joked. "Goodbye, Ashem. We will meet again." He said, before turning towards Jerusalem and walking in its direction.

Chapter 7

WELCOME AUDIENCES AT HOME, *to your morning world news. As always, I'm Jim Hassan. Today, we go live as all eyes are on Jerusalem and the scene of excitement at the site of the new temple, as the work is all but completed. The Emergency Military Organization, sent in by the Premier to protect the temple in accordance with the Israeli Green Peace Accord, continues its heavy presence in the area. The world remembers the day the horrendous attack on Israel began, just over three years earlier, as a large group of insurgents attempted to lay siege to Israel and its magnificent new temple. Many of us watched unknowingly, as the expected peace from that day was replaced by one of the bloodiest days in Israel's modern history. Sadly, it was also the day that those same insurgents attempted their cowardly assassination of the Premier; the man who had brokered Israel's peace treaty himself, as the world watched helplessly.*

In other news, the global food supply took yet another hit, as the last of the western ash continues to find its way to new nations, resulting in depleting oxygen levels, dying crops and low yields of vital grains. The last of the ash continues to fall despite the sudden loss of wind being reported across the globe. Scientists believe the strange occurrence, as well as the other global catastrophes are linked together somehow, as they reportedly continue to sweep through the nations. Making matters worse, the world-wide drought now marks its 40th day. This has caused some of the more dependable springs and wells throughout the middle east and Europe, to turn a bright red, garnering some to foolishly suggest a Biblical element to such things. Speaking with top strategist to the premier, Darrell Denotheo was quick to refute such notions as he has submitted the evidence of these occurrences to the United Nations as he continues to warn that those responsible for the great disappearing are also responsible for the plagues as well. According to Mr. Denotheo, his satellites definitively indicate there is continued extraterrestrial flight activity in Earth's atmosphere. If such can be proven, this would all but ensure that the Premier's emergency world-wide powers would continue. Mr. Denotheo believes the presence of extraterrestrial activity, may be caused by the United Nation's failures to act on the global emission initiative and the global banning of religious practices, as the occurrences, seem to align with that thinking. The Premier, and a UN delegate, are slated to visit Israel, to open the temple next Sunday, allowing for the return of the sacrifice of the red heifers, despite concerns that this could entice the world's domestic and foreign enemies, into an attack. How the current concerns will affect those plans, remains to be seen. We will keep you up to date on this and the growing speculation that the famed link18 will be made public, as we receive that information. From all of us here at the World News Network, that's what's happening in your world.

Chapter 8

MAYA SIGHED AND SHUT the TV off. She walked to the kitchen and placed two blueberry muffins into a bag, before walking out of the door. Ima, still shaken from the late night with Abi, remained locked in her room. Maya put her ear to Ima's door. She could hear that she was praying. She smiled, before turning to leave. She quietly walked out of the apartment and down the steps, to the alley. She came to the alley and called out loudly… "Mash'pekh?". She saw movement in the darkness at the end of the alley and made her way over. "Is that you, Mash?" she asked. But no one responded. "Mash Mash?" she called out again, before slowing her walk toward the person standing in the shadows. "Maya…" A voice suddenly whispered from within the shadow. Maya froze. She knew it wasn't Mash'pekh's voice. "Come to me, Maya. I have a secret to tell you." The voice whispered. Maya stood terrified. She called out to the shadow, "Who are you?". The shadow seemed to move, as it spoke… "I am one who was and is. A messenger of sorts. I have something wonderful to tell you. Do you want to know what it is?". Maya felt a chill on her skin. She started to tremble. She frantically stared into the moving shadow to try and see who was speaking. "Why can't I see you?" she asked nervously. Suddenly, two eyes illuminated from the shadows: their red stare, piercing into her mind. Maya screamed instantly, and turned to run away, but tripped over her feet. She fell to the ground and turned over to look back. The shadow suddenly rushed towards her, laughing. "My secret is…" the voice growled as it rushed towards Maya. Suddenly, a powerful glow emitted from the sky. Maya looked up to see what looked like beautiful white fire coming down upon the moving shadow, consuming it as it charged to her. The shadow was engulfed by the flames that disintegrated the darkness, revealing a bright and beautiful being inside. The engulfed being looked down at himself and sneered. It then looked angrily at Maya and screamed, before disappearing before her. Maya screamed in terror, as the blazing fire that had exposed it, extinguished on its own. She looked up helplessly and exhaled. "What the absolute..." she began to say when a frantic voice called out from behind her. "Maya. Are you alright, dear?". It was Mash'pekh who walked briskly to her side. "I'm so sorry you saw that, my child.".

Maya stared in horror at Mash'pekh. "What... what was that?" she asked, her voice barely able to carry her words. "It was a force of darkness that only now is beginning to show itself in this world." He replied. "You mean... Aliens? The ones who took all of those people and blew up the west?" She asked, while trembling. Mash'pekh smiled. "No, my dear. Those things you mentioned don't exist." He exclaimed as he helped Maya to her feet. Maya looked into her friend's eyes. She then began to sob. "I don't understand any of this. Mash, I talked to my brother last night. He told me he's now part of your group." Mash'pekh looked at Maya sympathetically and nodded. "He is. He is *very* special to the Lord, as are you." Maya continued to sob. "I just don't understand any of this, Mash. Please help me understand. How could we all be so easily fooled?" She begged. "Oh.... The deception of your generation is like no other deception. For Satan himself has come." he cried out with a loud sigh as he hugged Maya tight. Maya stepped back and stared at her friend. She took a breath and asked, "Was that Satan? Like, the actual devil?" She asked reluctantly. He smiled. "Oh no. That was just a slave to him. His name is Azul. He is a legion of tormentors, who once was a being of light. Sit down my child, and I will tell you what I can. Much more is coming, and you and your mother will need to decide your place in it all." Maya shook her head. "Ima? I don't think Ima will ever leave her room after everything Abi told us." She exclaimed. Mash'pekh sat down and pointed Maya to the curb next to him. Maya sat down and looked at him, her eyes filled with tears and confusion. As Mash'pekh sat beside her, he began to speak, but immediately turned to see a brown bag lying on the ground. He looked back at Maya and asked eagerly, "Is that for me?". The question broke Maya from her shock. She smiled as best as she could muster and rose to her feet and picked up the bag, before handing it to Mash'pekh. "I hope you enjoy them, Mash Mash. I literally almost died to give them to you." Mash'pekh laughed as he received the bag with gladness. "Oh, child. You are a gift!" he exclaimed joyfully. They sat together as each stared at the brick wall across from them. As Mash'pekh reached into the bag and grabbed one of the muffins, Maya took a breath. She turned and said, "Now tell me what the heck just happened and what I need to do."

Chapter 9

"He's here!" they yelled, as the black limousine, surrounded by many armored vehicles, pulled up to the ceremonial entrance of the temple, for its grand opening. The media in attendance turned their attention to the opening door of the vehicle, as a tall, regal-looking, brown-haired man emerged. His steely blue eyes gazed out at the adoring crowd. He smiled and waved heroically, drawing cheers from all in attendance. The affection from the crowd, was genuine. Regarded as one of the greatest men in all of history, the Premier was especially held as a hero to the Jewish people. It was his treaty that had brought about such lasting peace when it was forged immediately within the United Nations after the disappearing. The treaty ensured all nations would cease any hostility towards one and other and their resources were immediately pooled for a global, unified defense and deterrent. But what endeared him especially towards the Israeli nation, was his insistence that any treaty agreed upon, must also include permission and protection for Israel to build its long-awaited third temple. Also emerging from the same vehicle, and equally victorious looking, was none other than the illustrious Darrell Denotheo, the man whose technological advancements delivered a new era of hope, amidst the promised peace and security from the Premier. For the remaining world that wasn't affected by the destruction that engulfed the western nations shortly after the disappearing, a ceremonial opening and celebration of the temple was to be broadcast live in every home, across the world as a world-wide celebration. Both the Premier and Mr. Denotheo were also going to be attending the first public implantations of Mr. Denotheo's incredible triumph, the famed and long-awaited, "link18" program. link18 was long rumored to be made available free, to all Israeli government employees and military the day the Premier was slated to visit to celebrate the opening of the temple. The world stood anxious to see if such rumors were true.

link18, with its powerful combination of artificial intelligence and cerebral app-driven interface, was a rice-sized device, designed to be implanted into either the right hand or the forehead, for maximum interface. link18 offered its users the ability to regain their lost connectivity to each other, since the removal of internet went into effect, shortly after the disappearing, to control the surge in propaganda and misinformation that was engulfing the world. link18 also boasted a broad spectrum of neuro-uploads and accessibility, fusing the human body with advanced digital technology. It was designed to single-handedly manage every aspect of one's health, personal information, and social connectivity. The database for link18, was to be housed on the United National Database, where it was protected from hacks and malware by programs designed by Mr. Denotheo and the Premier. However, it was the new breakthrough update for link18, that was generating more buzz than all the rest combined. link18 was rumored to have successfully enhanced itself to treat the human body for illnesses it detected, as they were detected, rendering the need for traditional medicines and vaccines, void. The Premier, being the first patient ever to receive link18, underwent the emergency procedure after the unsuccessful attempt was made to assassinate him during the insurgency of Israel. Seemingly fully restored and enhanced, He was now considered the face of the program and, its biggest advocate. The two men stood victoriously together at the front steps of the new temple, as they met the feverish crowds with a warm smile and a wave.

Chapter 10

"I'D LIKE TO SAY a few words." The Premier said, rendering the crowd almost instantly silent. "Friends... The last time I stood here before you, we had designated this site as the place where a new temple would be constructed. At a time, where much of the world was still reeling from the sudden and unprovoked taking of our own in the great disappearance, I vowed to never let another soul slip through my fingers. I set my course towards peace and security, even as I was nearly alone, to follow such a bold direction. We all know the horrific events that occurred that day, not just to me personally, but to all of Israel. My efforts for global peace and security were met by an assassination attempt that almost took my life. Then, at the same time, the great land of Israel suffered an insurgent attack that left over twenty thousand innocent civilians dead, at the hands of religious zealots and terrorists. Nearly three and a half years have passed since that fateful day. I now stand before you thanks to the lifesaving efforts of my dear friend, Mr. Denotheo, and the incredible healing power of our new technology, which we will make available to Israel without charge, to commemorate this day!" The crowd cheered raucously for the Premier as he was applauded throughout the world, during the live broadcast. "Thank you. Thank you." The premier said, before adding.... "Not a day goes by that I don't use the memory of the disappeared and the fallen as motivation to enhance our way of life. Through this way, we have achieved relative peace. Removing the religious confines and their arbitrary rules that once divided us, we now celebrate our differences as a united world, free of our former shackles. It's this united front, combined with our efforts to continue our global climate pledges across the world, that no longer provoke our enemies beyond this world. They no longer see weakness and gullibility from Earth, as we remove the last of our society that holds t that archaic way of thinking and the danger it presents. No, our enemies afar see strength, now! They see unity! We cannot afford to step away from either of these. link18 is the next evolution in man's evolution." The crowd erupted with cheers and celebration. The Premier waited for their applause to subside, before continuing, saying… "These days friends, I'll admit…. I feel mechanical in nature. I'll admit, I don't totally feel like myself." The crowd that had been so loud and boisterous, began to quiet themselves. "I personally blame link18 for this." The Premier added, as he looked out to see the confusion on the faces of the crowd. The premier smiled and stepped around the podium before the crowd. Every eye watched in wonder as the man who had performed such miracles, was about to do. He lifted his arms into the sky, as the crowd looked on eagerly. Then, with his arms still raised, the Premier turned back towards where Mr. Denotheo was standing and nodded. He turned himself back towards the crowd and swiftly brought both arms down before him, in a pushing motion and cried out, startling the crowd. Suddenly, behind him came two powerful missiles that cracked out from the sky, just beyond the mountains. The crowd watched the speeding objects the Premier had brought forth with the power of his own arms. They screamed and howled approvingly, marveling at the sight. As the rockets flared throughout the sky, onlookers noticed they were screaming their way towards the temple, where the Premier stood. The crowd began to point and scream in terror at the incoming menace. The Premier looked around at the fearful crowd and smiled, calming them. The missiles howled across the sky, with great speed. As they did, the Premier raised his right hand above his head. Every eye watched in wonder as he then turned towards where the missiles were coming and put his right hand in the air, and screamed out, "Peace!", as he waived his hand down once more, just as he had done before. The missiles at once, exploded in midair, vaporizing instantly. The Premier turned back towards the people before him to see the awe written across their faces. "He can control weapons from his body!" one of the attendees cried out. The crowd gasped at what they just witnessed before all crying out in jubilation. "There's nobody like him!" they exclaimed before being overwhelmed in the celebration. The Premier raised his hands again, as he watched the crowd respond. Mystified by the power they just saw, a silence came over them as they watched, eagerly. The Premier smiled and said, "Make no mistake. I do not have interest in summoning weapons with just my hands and neither should any of you. My interest is deterring weapons from those hands that are not my own. Those who seek to disrupt peace. Those that seek to wield them against Mother Earth and her three and a half billion people." He said to thunderous applause, before continuing... "Any person who accepts link18 will be under the same protection you've witnessed today. We will be linked together, as a single people, protected from anything beyond the heavens or in them, that seeks to harm or oppress us. My promise to you, Israel is simple.... Never Again!" he shouted. The entire crowd roared and cheered at the incredible man's boldness. The Premiere then turned towards the entryway of the temple and followed by Mr. Denotheo and the ambassadors from the United Nations, with their security forces, entered the temple as the crowd continued to cheer from outside.

Chapter 11

MAYA RETURNED HOME, FRAZZLED after speaking with Mash'pekh. She walked in to see Ima sitting by herself at the dining table. Ima looked up and said somberly, "He's gone. He's not here.", referring to Abi. Maya closed the door to the apartment and sat at the dining table across from Ima, with neither saying anything to the other. It was as if Shiva had once more found there home. The weight of all they were given to process over the last few days, proved far more than they could handle. Suddenly, the silence was broken. "I knew when your father passed, that everything would change. I guess I didn't realize just how much." Ima said, her eyes fixed towards the windows where the sun was just beginning to shine through. Maya looked to her mother and nodded. "I've seen things I can't unsee, now. The reality of it all has been forced on me. I cannot unsee any of it. Believe me, I've tried." She said, as her eyes moved rapidly, while she recounted all that Abi and Mash'pekh had shared. She saw her brother's Bible still sitting on the coffee table from two nights before. She retrieved it and brought it back to the dining table. She opened the book to the page in Revelation, that Abi had led them to. "I need to see it again." She whispered. Ima turned towards her daughter and watched her large brown eyes widen further, as she sifted through the pages. "It has to be real." She said, her eyes being drawn up to her mother's. Ima nodded. "You're not being there at the temple this morning with your co-workers, told me how much you believe it." Ima said. "It isn't easy." Maya responded. "These things never are." Ima replied. "What about you?"

Maya asked her mother. Ima just sighed. Her eyes welled up. "My problem isn't how wrong this all seems, my dear, but how right. I've spent the last day and night praying to a God I had forgotten, asking for wisdom I've never had, like my son told me to." Ima said, tearfully. Maya's heart melted. "Ima..." she said, affectionally, before adding, "I've judged them my entire life – these Christians. I never saw anything that drew me in to them. I also don't remember ever looking, though. Never did I think I would join them. And never did I think Abi would either. I thought this would be one of the greatest days of my life. Like, actually getting to meet the Premier. I should be right there, right now. I thought I would have the link by days-end. I never pictured I would be doing...." This..." Maya pointed to the paper bag she had placed on the table. "I hope he at least enjoyed the muffins you made him." Ima said, as she reached for the empty bag and opened it. Inside the bag, Ima saw thousands of shekels, all lumped together in a large chaotic wad. She sighed, before saying, "Abi was right about the money Mash'pekh would give you, I see. Did he tell you how much it is or what it would be for?" She asked Maya. Maya sighed. "He said it was exactly enough to get us there and stocked up for the others." She replied. Ima nodded as she folded up the bag. "Then it is." She said stoically.

Maya and her mother began to pack up their things quickly, as Abi had instructed the night before when he revealed to them what they were called to do. "How long is the trip?" Maya asked. "4-5 hours." Ima responded, as she rifled through her drawers, sorting what clothes of hers to bring. "I'll pack light then." Maya said. "Pack everything! We're not coming back, dear." Ima replied, reminding her daughter of the plan. Maya paused for a moment and looked around. "Oh, that's right. We can't come back after to-day." She said, saddened by the revelation. "We won't want to." Ima declared as she packed up her personal belongings and piled them by the door. As the women finished, they loaded up items into the family's old truck, downstairs. They went back up to the apartment one last time.

Chapter 12

As THEY STEPPED INSIDE, they quietly looked around at the home that just a few years ago, had been filled with such love and joy. "I'll miss it." Maya said, as she put her arm around her mother. "Me too dear." Ima said as she rubbed her daughter's hand. Ima paused and then turned towards Maya, grabbing her face. "But it was never the same since he was taken." She said, firmly. Maya hugged her mother, as both sobbed. They turned and left the only apartment they had ever known, with a course set for the unknown. As they made their way out of the apartment complex, they hurried to their vehicle with the last of their belongings in tow. As Maya opened the rear door to the family's truck, a voice called to her.... "You listened!" She turned to see Abi jogging over to where they were parked. Ima ran to her son and hugged him frantically. "My son. My son! Are you coming with us?" She asked eagerly. Abi shook his head. "I can't. Not right now, at least. I have to stay in Jerusalem until it's over." He said to the disappointment of his mother. Maya came over and hugged her brother. "He told me he talked with you. Are you ok? Do you understand?" Abi asked Maya, referring to Mash'pekh. "I don't know that I understand anything right now. But I'm doing what he said. And just so you know, I won't take the link now that I know what it really is." Maya assured her brother. Abi smiled. "Praise God. That was one of my prayers, Maya. I didn't fully realize what it was either until I read it for myself and saw the numbers." He said. "Me too. I was totally fooled." Maya replied. "The logo has three sixes, clearly. I was just more focused on the number eighteen, I think. But everyone will know today, huh?" she replied. "Yes, they will." Abi said as he helped load a small box into the car. "That's why you guys have to get to the firs stop before Petra, as quickly as possible and with the cargo he said was waiting." Maya nodded at her brother's instruction. "Man…. We were normal just a few weeks ago." She said, giggling. "You were never normal." Abi quipped. Maya smiled. "I love you, creep." She said as she hugged her brother once more. Ima also joined the hug. "Me too, my precious boy. Me too." Ima looked at Abi, staring deep into his eyes. "Now go and be what the Lord has called you to be." "Yes ma'am" He responded, tearfully. "Be careful, Abi. We won't be able to text or call each other after today. But please know we will be praying for you." Abi nodded, before saying, "Make sure you stop first at the place in Adassiyah that he told you about. They will have everything you need. Be careful and just give them the bag. Give them everything he gave you.". Maya nodded. "I will. I promise." She said. Maya and her mother then got into the truck. She backed out of the parking garage, stopped, and took one last look at her brother Abi. A lifetime of memories filled her mind, as she wondered to herself if she would ever see her brother again.

Chapter 13

ABI TURNED AND STARTED to walk towards the temple. He looked down the alley where he had first met Mash'pekh and saw the alley was much darker now that it had been emptied. He smiled as he recalled the first time he came across the incredible old man, the day he chose to cut through the alleyway, after school. He recalled seeing a small group of young men being captivated by the teachings of Mash'pekh, who to him, was just a random homeless man. He remembered that fateful day, listening in, unbeknownst to anyone there. That was the day he heard mentioned the name that had all but been outlawed; the name "Jesus.". He recalled feeling angry when he first heard it, as he waited for the man to stop speaking, vowing in his mind to confront the old hobo, as soon as everyone had left. He believed at the time, the foolish young men who were listening, were putting their lives and the lives of everyone else in grave danger. As the man's sermon concluded, the young men each embraced him, before dispersing from the alley. Abi saw his chance, but before he could jump out to confront the old man, he heard a voice call out to him… "You can come out now." Startled, Abi peeked out to see that the old homeless man was speaking to him. Abi remembered being confused. "How did you see me?" He asked the old man. "I see a great deal." The old man responded, with a smile. Abi though, quickly returned to his anger. "Do you see another disappearing? Because that's what old fools like you who talk about religion and Jesus, are going to bring on the rest of us." He said. Abi cringed at the thought, as he remembered the angry words, he spoke to Mash'pekh that day. He remembered his anger and words didn't come from a place of concern for the world or another disappearing, but they were just anger from being afraid. As he would come to understand later, it was the kind of consuming anger that many who walked the world's path, developed. He recalled the moment Mash'pekh shook him from his understanding, when he responded as such, saying "Young man, you are angry about a great many things, but none of them have any bearing on what I have spoken. You fear my words and yet the reasons you give aren't the reasons you speak. This did not come from your parents, so the question is, where and when did you lose yourself to such fear?" Abi remembered being silenced when those words were said. They cut him deeply. Yet still, he remembered his pride was how he responded, when he replied, "What am I angry about, hobo?". That was the moment Abi learned there was something very different about Mash'pekh. The "hobo" proceeded to tell him everything he was *really* angry about, to the shock of Abi. He recalled the loss of Abi's father and even knew his Father's name. Mash'pekh spoke of how losing friends to the disappearing had taken their toll on his otherwise gentle heart. He spoke gently of Abi's discomfort towards what the world was saying was the cause of the disappearing. Abi recalled feeling as if he were going to faint at the truthful Revelations from the old man he had only accidentally stumbled upon. After a few vulnerable moments though, Abi remembered once more trying to hide his shock at what was said, under a thin veil of sarcasm... "So, you're a prophet, eh? Tell me more Moses. Tell me!" he remembered saying jokingly. "I can tell you that I'm not Moses." He remembered a chuckling Mash'pekh respond. As he thought back on that day, he rekindled the wonder of the experience, the further he spoke with Mash'pekh. He didn't recall the moment the wall of his pride fell, but he remembered who it was who reached into the rubble to pull him out. The more he would be willing to hear, the more he wanted to hear more from Mash'pekh. And it was those many words that continued to bring Abi back, thirsting for more. Abi smiled at the thought of Mash'pekh many teachings and remembered how each of the moments culminated to him making a decision; taking Jesus as his Lord and savior, being baptized in an alley by a man he originally set out to confront. Abi smiled brightly at the thought, as he made his way to the temple grounds.

As he came to the barriers that divided the temple grounds from the public, he saw one of his fellow believers, waiting for him. "Tyrus!" he called out. Tyrus was standing at the corner of the barriers, where a small security entrance into the temple grounds was opened. Tyrus turned and waved to his friend. Abi jogged to Tyrus and the two embraced. "Are they here?" Abi asked. "Not yet, but soon." Tyrus replied as he looked around to see if anyone was watching them. "The brothers have made it through Jerusalem. Tevah met with the leaders and was making his way from there. All of Israel will know." He replied joyfully. Abi smiled, as he recounted those exact prophetic words from Mash'pekh. "No turning back now!" Tyrus quipped. As the two young men waited in the early hours of the day, Tevah and Mash'pekh suddenly came into view. They walked carefully around the first set of barriers, just outside of where Abi and Tyrus were standing as they slowly made their way to them. Abi watched eagerly, as Tevah came into view. "So that's Tevah, huh?" He asked. Tyrus smiled, before replying, "I've only ever heard stories. I was beginning to wonder if he was a real person.". "I'm sure his people wondered that about Mash'pekh." Abi replied, confidently. The two elderly men entered the barriers leading to where Abi and Tyrus stood. Mash'pekh smiled. "My boys, you made it! Praise His name!" he said with a smile, as he embraced each of them. Tevah came up and embraced them as well. "I've heard wonderful things. And you will now see WONDERFUL things!" Tevah exclaimed warmly. As the four men stood watching through the small opening of the security entrance, their eyes stayed fixed on the armed guards, who were standing at the temple's entry point. "The Lord forgive them." Mash'pekh said. "Indeed!" replied Tevah. Abi looked at Tyrus, before turning to Mash'pekh and asked, "What's going to happen to them?". Tevah and Mash'pekh turned towards each other with a somber look. "Sadly, their fate was sealed when they took the mark." Mash'pekh said, referring to link18. "I thought that only the premier and his group had link18?" Tyrus asked. Tevah turned and replied, "My son, many have already taken it, unbeknownst to Israel. A great deception is upon this world. Today is the first step in light coming upon the darkness to expose its works." Mash'pekh nodded. "Indeed." he said, agreeingly. "What do you want us to do, once you go in?" Abi asked the two. "You will be witnesses to what transpires. Afterwards, you both will stay here in town at Tyrus's home in the city square. The Lord will then come upon you with instructions." Tevah said. "The world will be thirsty for truth, but not at first. We will them something today that will change their hearts and further separate the wheat from the tares. Then, those chosen ones will further that message, until the coming of the Lord." Mash'pekh added. Abi, reluctantly pointed to himself. "Yes, you, Abi." Mash'pekh replied. Abi nodded, though neither he nor Tyrus understood. "No matter what, do no flee. Do not fear them. After today, Israel will be transformed. After today, the harvest will begin." Tevah responded, his eyes now fixed on the guards. Abi looked at Tyrus with widened eyes. Tyrus looked to Abi with the same shocked look.

Chapter 14

"GET OUT OF MY home, heretic!" shouted the heavy-set man, as he threw a plate against his wall. "You let these fools into our home?" He cried out to his eldest daughter, Noni. "Abba, they are only speaking what we have been asking..." a distraught Noni replied. "It's blasphemous!" Noni's father screamed. "All of this religious talk. Are you trying to make my family disappear?" He demanded from the men. Noni's mother stood up from the table. "If disappearing is what you're concerned about, then you can't be concerned about blasphemy as well, Thomas!" she exclaimed to her irate husband. Thomas was befuddled at his wife's retort. "You see? Look how you have now divided my family against me!" Is this what your Jesus would do? Divide families? Have you no shame?" He asked the young visitors. "Sir, my name too, is Tomas." One of them said humbly. "And my only aim here is for you to know the truth of what's happened and the truth of what's coming." Tomas said. "And his friend here, Sif, was showing us even in Torah where what they're saying can be seen, Abba." Noni added. But Thomas was still too irate to listen. "It's blasphemy!" He screamed as he threw more plates against his wall. "Time to go." Sif exclaimed, as Tomas nodded agreeingly, as both moved with his friend to the door. Noni ran to see them out; her father still breaking dishes in the kitchen. "I'm so sorry!" she said to the men as they walked out of the home. "No apology necessary. We don't come with easy news to hear." Tomas responded. "But please, make sure you watch today's live coverage of the temple visit, this afternoon. About 2:00

pm." Added Sif. "It's not easy to even ask this but.... Are you guys' terrorists?" She asked, drawing laughter from the men. "I'm so sorry." Noni said, embarrassed by her question. "The last home we visited; they asked if we were aliens trying to make more people disappear. Don't be embarrassed, Noni." Tomas assured her. Just then, a scream from the kitchen. "Noni! Get away from them and get back in here!" Thomas yelled as he flailed his hands in the air. "Go in peace, Noni." Sif whispered as the two young men watched Noni return to her quarreling house at the insistence of her furious father. From the street, Sif and Tomas could hear their yelling from the corner of the road. "Why is it always the last house, that erupts on us?" Asked Sif, jokingly. "You would prefer it be the first house?" Tomas replied, garnering a grin from his friend. "Good point." Sif responded. As they made their way to the edge of the town, they caught up with Danny and another young man named Matthew. "How did you do, gentlemen?" Tomas asked. Danny, with a look of exhaustion, raised both hands to give a "thumbs up". "It's just about finished. All of these homes have been hit by our first and second waves a few days ago. We're just amplifying the message a bit." Matthew said, as each looked around at the many homes. "If it wasn't already, today's broadcast will be the most watched event in the world." Sif said. "Do you guys know what they're planning to do?" Matthew asked. Each of the men just shrugged. "They never told us." Tomas replied. "They only said to share Christ and get everyone we could to watch today." Replied Danny. "And it appears we have done that." Tomas added, proudly. The men agreed. Like all who were sent out, they had seen the hatred and disbelief among their people. Though, as Tevah explained to them, it was a product of great deception and the fear that deception evokes in people's hearts. Tevah did not blame Israel or the world beyond them for their disbelief. He always blamed the invisible enemy, as he called him. He taught the young men to always be ready to contend with Satan and to never let their guards down to him. Few teachers those days would dare entertain a lesson about Jesus, let alone Satan, with unsanctioned religion considered a severely punishable crime, given its mass-implication in the disappearing.

But Tevah, always taught about the power of darkness, the prince of this world held. He said it was important for anyone in a war, to know how your enemy thinks and attacks. His words had always made tremendous sense, which is why listeners seemed to flock to him in such large numbers. The men recalled many of his teachings on their way to their group's rendezvous point, having completed their assignment. The men set out eager to meet with their fellow disciples just outside the city of Jericho, which was to be the location for half of the group to meet.

They came to the large reserve, where they finally rested from their travel. Danny, started to build a firepit, as he began to set up meals for the incoming groups. In the distance, young men began to appear from multiple directions. "They're coming." Yelled Sif. Tomas stood up and looked out towards the horizon. He saw young men by the hundreds, coming from each direction of Israel. As the visitors made their way into the camp, they were greeted by Tomas, who was eager to hear of their victories. Tomas was amazed at the success each group had but found it even more amazing when he recalled Tevah had prophesied it would happen this way. The numbers of men joining the camp continued to increase over the next few hours, until there were no more set to arrive. Danny returned to Tomas with the final count. "Two short of seventy-two thousand!" he exclaimed. "Just as we were told." He added. Tomas smiled. "Everything we're seeing. All these prophecies coming to life. I can think of no place I'd rather be, brothers." He said. As he said it, some of the leaders of the groups came to join Tomas and his team. "Has anyone heard from Ashem yet?" Tomas asked. Matthew came to the group with one of the late-arriving members. "Him…. He's been to Ashem's camp just beyond the valley. This is Dante" Matthew said, as he introduced the young man. The young men all somewhat paused as they looked at Dante. "That doesn't sound like a Hebrew name…". Sif said skeptically. "I'm sorry brothers, I don't have the DNA testing to show you that justifies my lineage. What I do have is the spirit of the living God in my heart thanks to the grace given me by my Lord, Jesus Christ." He added. "Amen!" the men throughout the camp began to say as Dante's spirit had been tested and found welcomed. Tomas embraced the man. "Welcome, Dante! You came from Ashem's camp?" "Yes! About a day's hike through the ridge." Dante replied, pointing towards the mountain in the distance. "Good. Rest up with us. We'll leave under the cover of nightfall." He said as the leaders then each returned to their groups and shared the news.

Chapter 15

MAYA TURNED OFF THE highway. "This is our first exit?" She asked Ima, who was holding the map. "Oh, are you sleeping?" she asked her mother sarcastically, as she watched the women looking out her window. "Oh no…" Ima replied, before adding, "I may never sleep again! No, I was just praying.". Maya smiled. "Anything you want to share?" she asked. Ima didn't respond. Maya, doing her best to watch the road and look at her mother, asked again. "Ima?". Ima sighed. "For truth, my dear." Ima said, reluctantly. "You don't have to be embarrassed by that, Ima. This is new for me too." Maya assured her mother. "Well, I…" Ima began to say, when suddenly the vehicle jumped. "Whoa!" Maya yelled, as she turned to see the road had suddenly gone from concrete to now rocky sand. She applied the brakes and brought the vehicle to a stop. "Are you ok?" she asked Ima. "I'm fine, fine. But that won't help my efforts to sleep, dear." Ima quipped. Maya looked out at the dirt road ahead. "Did we take a wrong turn?" she asked, looking at the map with Ima. "No. This is the way. We just keep going." Ima said confidently. Maya looked at her mother, puzzled by her assertion. She stuck her head out of her window and looked back behind them, to see the road had ended well behind them. She then looked forward. "I hope this old girl can take this road, Ima. It's gonna get really hot, really quick if we break down in the middle of nowhere, out here." "Have faith, dear." Ima said, as she smiled towards her daughter. Maya squinted her eyes at the comment. "Take it easy, Elijah…" she said, garnering a laugh from her mother. "I didn't know I was with a prophet this whole time." Maya added, as she put the vehicle into drive and began to move forward down the rocky road.

As the vehicle continued down the hazardous stretch of road, the desert surroundings unnerved Maya. "We're really going deep into this." She said softly. "Don't let it take your peace, dear." Ima said. In the distance, she saw a large rock formation begin to take shape through the beaming sunlight. It was the base of the mountains, the exact location Mash'pekh had described to her. "This is it!" Maya declared, her nervousness giving way. Ima squinted as she stared at the rocky base of the mountain foothills. "Did they carve it from stone or something?" She said, as she marveled. "No, he said it's behind these stones, hidden." Maya replied. As Maya navigated carefully around the large boulders, her car jostled, as the landscape continued to push the limits of the family's truck. "C'mon girl, c'mon." She whispered. As she looked at the console, she saw a yellow light flashing. "Oh no…" she said. "What?" Ima asked. "The engine light has been flashing." Maya responded, before adding, "I was too distracted to notice.". Ima leaned over to see the light for herself. The truck began to jerk and vibrate, as Maya brought the speed to an idle. "Not good." Maya said as her worry quickly returned. "Not good at all." She yelled, her frustrations giving way. "Maya!!!!" Ima screamed, shaking her from her thoughts, as she turned to see her mother pointing towards the front of the vehicle. Maya looked up and came to an abrupt stop. There before her, stood a young man with an assault rifle pointed towards their vehicle. "Oh my gosh…" Maya said, as she stopped the truck and immediately grabbed her mother's hand.

Chapter 16

"PUT YOUR HANDS UP and get out of your truck, now!" The young man shouted. Maya froze. "Do as he says." Ima whispered as both women nervously reached for their doors to exit. Maya began to shake as she watched the young man leer at her, once she got out; his weapon locked on her. "We didn't do anything; we just went the wrong way." She said, trembling. "Quiet!" the young man ordered. Maya shook, frightened by his yell. "On the ground!" He yelled. Maya looked over to Ima and nodded, as both women slowly and carefully laid themselves down on the hot and rocky sand. Maya and Ima both winced at the burning feel of the sun-scorched ground. Maya looked under the truck, towards where she could see Ima laying, before looking forward towards where the young man still stood. The sun light that protruded through the mountains, prevented her from seeing clearly in his direction, adding to her nervousness. Suddenly, she heard the young man whistle. From behind the adjacent rocks, more people emerged, each holding rifles, pointed towards Maya and her mother. They came out and ran to where Maya and her mother laid; the rattling of their weaponry echoing fearfully throughout the mountain's base. Maya screamed as they ran toward her, frightened by the sight. "Quiet!" the young man yelled, again causing Maya to jump once more, as she cowered helplessly before the group. The people came over to her side of the vehicle. "Search it." She heard one of them, a deep-voiced male, say. Maya suddenly remembered the money Mash'pekh had given her. "Please don't take our stuff!" she begged.

"I said shut up!" she heard the young man call out. She looked over once more towards her mother and could see the legs of those guarding her side. She saw each person was wearing black boots, with what looked to be military fatigue-style pants draping over them. As she lay near her truck, she heard the axels begin to jostle, as the people were rummaging through it. "Whoa…" she heard one of them say. She heard another loud jostle from the truck, as one of the fatigue-clad figures jumped down, before walking over to where the young man stood. She did her best to see what was happening, but the sunlight still blocked most of her view. She was able to see the person going over to him was carrying the bag of money, Mash had given her. She began to weep. "No!" she whispered. "Shut up!" she heard a female's voice from behind her say, as she was startled. Out of the corner of her eye, she could see a person standing to her left, pointing their rifle towards her. She was terrified. She looked and saw the young man rummage through the bag with the person who had brought it to him, before looking up towards her and pointing. He gave orders to the person behind Maya, but she could not hear what was said. She saw the young man hand his rifle to the man who was holding the bag and walk towards Ima. Then, she saw him pull a pistol from his side, as he made his way to her side of the truck. "Ima" she yelled. Immediately, she felt the barrel of a rifle touch the back of her head. "One more word…" the woman behind her said. She sobbed, helplessly. She looked over to see Ima was no longer laying in the ground but being lifted from it. She saw three sets of feet making their way around the truck and over to her. "Get her up." The young man shouted, as Maya immediately felt herself being hoisted upwards from the ground. She could feel the barrel that she previously felt against her head, now in the small of her back, as she was stood up. She saw the young man coming closer, with a tear-soaked and dirt-covered Ima, and another man. Both men had military-style clothing, with insignias on their shirts. She squinted and saw the insignia they were wearing had a similar pyramid-shaped image as what she remembered the branding of link18 having. As she looked closer though, she didn't see link18 written in the pyramid.

Instead, she saw the words "OWL", written in large golden letters. Just below the pyramid, she saw an insignia. It read "One World Law".

Chapter 17

MAYA DIDN'T KNOW WHO they were but watched the men aggressively lead Ima over to where she was now standing. She saw her mother's hands had been bound with rope. She began to sob at the sight of her mother, tied up, frail and distraught. She heard more footsteps coming from behind her. Then, she felt her shaking fists suddenly grabbed as her arms were pulled behind her. Someone then, started to fasten her wrists together. She sobbed heavily. The young man stopped a few feet from Maya and brandished his pistol. He held Ima close to him and looked at Maya. He grinned wickedly, and with a heavy Arabic accent, he asked her…. "Do you want your mother to die today?" Maya froze. She continued to sob, as she shook her head in response. "Please…" she groveled, before pleading, "Take the money and let us go." She immediately felt herself thrown to the ground. "Maya, oh my goodness!" Ima screamed, helplessly. "Shut up!" she heard one of the men say as the young man clinched the woman's shoulder tightly. Ima was helpless to help her daughter. Maya didn't have a chance to get her bearings before she once again felt herself violently hoisted up. She sobbed, as she screamed out, "What do you want from us!" The man smiled. His eyes squinted as he snickered. He paused for a moment and then spoke… "Say Jesus is a lie." he ordered to Maya. Maya was shocked and caught by surprise by the request. "What?" she asked, with confusion. The young man smiled, before saying, "Ok…". She watched as he immediately put the barrel of his pistol to Ima's head. "Say Jesus is a lie!" he repeated, his eyes showing a fierce anger, as his tone became more commanding. Maya's mind raced, before realizing what the man was asking. Maya looked at her mother and saw the frightened woman, soaked in a combination of tears and dust. Ima slowly shook her head to Maya. Maya sobbed. "Please..." She said, at which point the young man yelled in frustration, causing Maya and Ima to jump with fear. "I told you..." he said as he cocked his pistol. "No!" Maya screamed as she raised her hands outward. "No, please." She begged. "Say it!" the man demanded once more, his thunderous voice echoing out into the desert surrounding them, as he thrusted his pistol against Ima's temple. Ima closed her eyes and sobbed, helplessly. Maya turned her eyes towards the young man and did her best to muster words... "Jesus..." Maya whispered, while shaking. "Jesus is..." She muttered a little louder, among the heavy sobs. The man's eyes widened. "Say it." He said coldly, in a muted tone. Maya shook. She quieted her sobs and composed herself. She looked once more at Ima to see she was shaking her head, subtly. Maya's eyes turned back again to the young man. She cleared her throat and breathed out. She opened and closed her hands, releasing the sweat that had accumulated in them while lying in the hot sand, under duress. She exhaled and said, "Jesus is Lord.". The young man's eyes widened. Then, with the pistol against Ima's temple, he pulled the trigger.

Chapter 18

THE PISTOL "CLICKED" AND didn't fire. Maya gasped and screamed, "IMA!". Then, noticing the gun hadn't fired, Ima's eyes opened, as she looked confusingly towards Maya. She gasped, exhaling every breath she had been holding. Maya looked fearfully towards her mother, before turning and looking immediately towards the young man. She didn't know if the gun had misfired, or if he somehow might've forgot to load it. She stood up, still bound, and ran quickly to her mother's side, falling to the ground beside her. "Are you ok?" she yelled to Ima, as both women sobbed, uncontrollably. Ima, her arms still bound, did her best to put her body against her daughter's. "Do it." They then heard the young man say to the older man standing to his side. The man walked over to the women, brandishing a large knife. "No!" Maya yelled as she did her best to shield her mother. "No!" Ima yelled. The man placed his knife behind Maya and mad a swift ripping motion up her back, as Maya just stared into her mother's eyes. "Maya! Oh my God!" screamed Ima. Maya's eyes widened. Suddenly, her arms swung forward; her ropes having been severed. Ima breathed in an immediate sigh of relief. The man walked around Maya and very gently cut Ima's ropes. The two women embraced each other once more, neither caring about the hot sand they were still sitting in. Suddenly, Maya felt a hand on her shoulder. She looked up and saw the young man, with his hand extended out to her. Her eyes widened. She pushed his hand away and fell back into the sand, desperate to get away from him. Ima crawled over to her and held

Maya still. She picked something up from the where the two were laying, as suddenly, Maya felt a cool liquid on her lips. She saw her mother was holding a bottle of water to her mouth, desperate to get her daughter to drink. "Where did that come from?" Maya asked confusingly, as she reluctantly gulped the liquid. "He was trying to give it to you." Ima said, pointing towards the young man, who was kneeling next to them. Maya looked at him and scowled. "What? What do you want?" she asked him, exhausted and befuddled. The young man smiled; his eyes now showing a peaceful gaze, far removed from the wickedness she saw just a few moments earlier. "Baptism is never an easy thing." He said, before quickly adding, "Especially when its baptism by fire." Maya just stared at the man, confused and angry. She looked around at the others who were there and could see a group of nine people; seven men and two women, as each had begun to remove their masks. "Are you going to kill us?" Maya asked. The young man paused for a moment. He looked around his group and smiled. "I'm giving you cold water in a hot desert. I assure you; my goal is to keep you alive and moving forward." he said. Maya looked around at the faces to see the men and women appeared to be Americans. She looked over to Ima, who she saw looking equally confused. The group helped the befuddled women to their feet. One of the women there, a blonde woman with light blue eyes, walked over to Ima and began to brush the dirt and sand from her. She took a rag from her vest and softly wiped the tears from Ima's face. "Let's get you cleaned up, Ima." the woman whispered warmly. Ima, no longer shaking, responded softly…. "Bless you, child.". The blonde women smiled. She looked at Maya, who watched puzzled by the sudden show of kindness. "I'm Jessica. I'd imagine you both have some questions for us." She said.

Chapter 19

MAYA WATCHED AS JESSICA motioned to the group in a circular pattern with her finger. The fatigue-clad group began to move Maya and Ima's truck towards one of the sand dunes, as both women watched. "What are you doing?" Maya asked, still in shock from all that had transpired. "We need to clear this location. They're watching for anything that would give away our position." Jessica replied as she watched the group finish moving the vehicle out of view. "Cover it all!" she yelled. The group picked up from the ground, a large swath of dirty canvas-like material and began to cover the truck as best as they could. They then began to empty it of what the two women had packed for the journey. Jessica motioned the young man who Maya and her mother had first encountered, over to where she was standing. "Justin, have the team take their belongings inside." Justin nodded, before making his way over to the group to retrieve the items. The team then carried the belongings a few yards beyond where Maya and her mother had first encountered Justin, before they seemed to somehow disappear into the rocks. "Let's get you inside." Jessica said, her eyes fixed out towards the horizon, as she held her hand out to Ima. Ima grabbed Jessica's hand and with her help, stepped over the rocky terrain, before finding better footing along a sandy path. She then turned and held her hand out to Maya. "C'mon, Maya..." she said, as her eyes drew back from the horizon, onto Maya. Maya looked up at Jessica and breathed deeply. She pushed her hand away and stood up on her own, refusing Jessica's help. Jessica smiled. "I wouldn't take my hand after all of that, either." She said understandingly. Maya joined her mother and hugged her once more, as Jessica began to walk towards where the others disappeared into. "Are you ok?" Maya whispered to Ima, as the two watched Jessica. "I'm ok, dear." Ima replied as she wiped dust from Maya's face. Then, they heard Jessica call out from the distance, "Follow me.". Maya looked at Ima. She then looked around the horizon at the vast mountains and deserts. "We don't have a choice, dear." Ima said, as she watched her daughter plan an escape, she knew would be fruitless.". Maya and Ima followed Jessica, reluctantly. The women walked together past the large rock where they first encountered Justin, before coming to another swatch of dirty canvas, at the rock's base Jessica bent down and moved the cloth, revealing a small opening. She held the cloth up and pointed Maya and Ima towards the opening, with her head. Maya froze. "What's in there?" she asked, refusing to move forward with assurance. "Hope." Jessica replied, as she once more motioned the two women to enter. Ima grabbed Maya's hand. "Stay with me, dear." She said to Maya. Maya clutched her mother's hand tightly, as both women entered, followed by Jessica. As Jessica entered in and dropped the canvas cloth behind them, she said, "Welcome to the Oasis.".

Chapter 20

THE WOMEN'S EYES ADJUSTED to show a narrow, underground corridor. Though poorly lit, Maya could see that it stretched out a long way. Maya stared at the dark, narrow pathway before her and sighed. "You've got to be kidding me…" She whispered, frustratingly, when she was startled by a sudden latching sound, from behind her. She turned to see Jessica, sealing a steel door that was hidden under the canvas they entered through. "Claustrophobic, huh?" Jessica said with a smile, as she leapt down from the stoop, where the doorlatch was. Maya scoffed at the comment and refused to answer. "Oh yes!" Ima replied to Jessica to the annoyance of her daughter. Maya scowled towards her mother. Jessica smiled. "I am too. You're in good company." She said cheerfully, as she shouldered her rifle and began to lead the women through the dark and narrow corridor. As she walked ahead, she held her right hand up, running it along the wall. "This should help some…" Jessica said as she flipped a switch from the darkness of the tunnel. Suddenly, the ceiling faintly illuminated, giving more sight to the tunnel's surroundings. Maya looked around to see the hollowed-out pathway. It seemed endless. "Oh…. I'm not sure that helps at all." Ima quipped as the daunting space came to view, revealing the massive depth of the tunnel. "It'll be ok." Jessica assured them as she began to walk through it. She turned and smiled. "Have you eaten yet?" She asked, before turning and walking down the tunnel. Maya and Ima, without any choice, followed her, cautiously. "What is the Oasis?" Ima asked, as they walked behind Jessica. "It was one of the old insurgent tunnels used to stage the attacks on Israel after the disappearing. It's one of only two places left that *they* don't know about." She replied. "Who doesn't know about it?" Maya asked, confused. "OWL." Jessica replied. "Wait, I thought *you* were OWL?" Maya responded, becoming increasingly confused. Jessica laughed. "No. We kill OWLS and take their feathers." She said boldly as she turned playfully and grabbed the collar of her shirt, before turning back to continue walking. "Goodness..." Ima replied, taken back by the comment. "What's so bad about OWL?" Ima asked. Jessica stopped and turned towards the women, which made Maya and Ima stop walking. "Do you all not know who OWL is?" she asked. "No." Maya responded. "Oh, Israel..." Jessica said, as she looked down. "They don't even know yet." She added. "Know what?" Maya asked. Jessica sighed. "OWL is the one world law. A secret military force the premier has been building since he was given his power. They've superseded the United Nations military force and the Green Peace Coalition. They answer only to the Premier and he uses them for his bidding." Jessica said to the women's shock. "What? How do we not know about this?" Ima responded skeptically, looking towards Maya. Jessica shook her head. "Because Israel is the last to get the mark." Jessica responded. Maya paused for a moment and thought. "link18?" she asked. Jessica breathed deeply. "That's what they first called it." She said. "First? What's it called now?" May asked. Jessica looked up. "It's the mark of the beast, Maya." She responded sadly. Maya squinted. "I thought the mark of the beast was supposed to be three sixes?" she protested. Jessica shook her head. She reached into her vest and pulled a small pocket-sized book from it. She opened it and began to read from the book... "Revelation 13, Chapter one...

[11] *Then I saw another beast rising out of the earth. It had two horns like a lamb and it spoke like a dragon.* [12]*It exercises all the authority of the first beast in its presence, and makes the earth and its inhabitants worship the first beast, whose mortal wound was healed.* [13]*It performs great signs, even making fire come down from heaven to earth in front of people,* [14]*and by the signs that it is allowed to work in the presence of the beast it deceives those who dwell on*

earth, telling them to make an image for the beast that was wounded by the sword and yet lived.[15] And it was allowed to give breath to the image of the beast, so that the image of the beast might even speak and might cause those who would not worship the image of the beast to be slain.[16] Also it causes all, both small and great, both rich and poor, both free and slave, to be marked on the right hand or the forehead,[17] so that no one can buy or sell unless he has the mark, that is, the name of the beast or the number of its name.[18] This calls for wisdom: let the one who has understanding calculate the number of the beast, for it is the number of a man, and his number is 666.

Chapter 21

MAYA AND IMA GASPED at what Jessica had read aloud. Jessica nodded. "I know. Right under all our noses." She said, before turning and continuing through the tunnel. Maya turned towards her mother, frozen. "Remember Abi stopped reading to us right there…" She reminded Ima. Ima nodded. "I believed him about the Premier, but Ima…" she said, before giving way to shock. "I almost took it so willingly. Like…. I was excited about it and everything." She said, shocked by the weight of the sudden revelation. Ima held her hand and tried to pull her forward. "But you didn't, dear." She said, confidently as she nudged her daughter from her shock. "That's right!" Jessica yelled out from deep within the tunnel as she took continued to move forward. The women made their way through the vast tunnel and then came to a doorway entrance. Jessica pounded on the door seven times. The large steel door, popped free as dust and sand fell from its swing, revealing a brilliant light beyond the entrance. Jessica waved the two women through as she entered. Maya and Ima walked through the doorway as Jessica stood inside, waiting to latch the door behind them. When they entered, they were both taken aback by what they saw. They were standing on a steel stairwell, high above a massive cavern of sorts, overlooking a small arsenal of military weaponry and supplies. "My God" Ima whispered as she stared out towards the array of artillery, vehicles, and equipment. "It looks like another incursion is being planned." She whispered to Maya. "Almost." Jessica said, her voice straining as she sealed off the large steel door behind them. "Luckily, we found it before it could be used by Israel's enemies." She said confidently. As she made her way down the stairs, Maya, emboldened by the earnest conversation with Jessica, asked "Why did you do that to us back there? What was that?". Jessica turned and faced Maya. "We needed to be sure. I'm sorry you went through that. I really am. But try to understand... These are the most perilous moments in our world's history. People disappearing, drought, earthquakes, famines, rivers turning to blood... Being sure the Lord is with someone is no longer as easy as asking. For the sake of everything we're about to do, we have to be very sure of things, like who people are." said Jessica. Maya scoffed. "What? Did you think a couple of lost women were going to steal all your weapons?" she asked sarcastically, as she pointed her finger towards the arsenal below the staircase." Jessica shook her head and stared coldly at Maya. "Maya, try to understand, we're up against a level of deception that has infiltrated every form of government as well as civilian infrastructure our world has created. We don't have the means to vet people like we once did. This outpost is the last of its kind and only still exists, because a random Israeli citizen was kind enough to point us to it, after our home country was wiped off the map." She said boldly, her voice beginning to raise. Maya froze. "So, you all *are* American..." Ima said, as she looked towards the group at the bottom of the stairway, with compassion. "That's right." Jessica replied as she looked over the banister of the staircase, out towards her team.

Chapter 22

JESSICA TURNED TOWARDS THE women and from the top of the steel staircase, recalled to Maya and Ima, the painful set of events that led to their being there…. "We were marines, deployed to the area during the Israeli and Arab peace summit. We received intel that an incursion was being planned the same week as the peace summit. We were deployed and stationed, completely focused on keeping the peace in the Middle East, when the disappearing happened. There wasn't time to gather ourselves. Over half of the American military was taken in the blink of an eye. No warnings, outside of a book we were all too busy to read. America was no longer a superpower. Those of us that remained, did our best to regroup, but then the incursion happened, and the assassination attempt of the Premier right after. As if well-planned, we were suddenly cut off from each other and the world, with an American-sized target on our backs. Soon, bounties were being placed on all American soldiers and citizens. We were at constant. My unit was one of the last remaining units in Israel. After heavy losses, we were cornered in the valleys surrounding this place, when out of nowhere, a stranger appeared. He told us what had happened. What *REALLY* happened. It wasn't foreign invaders or our climate. It was the Rapture. And it was right under our noses. As we carried along the belongings of those who disappeared from our initial group, we found that many of them had Bibles. This was only days before Bibles were made illegal by the United Nations. The stranger led us through the chapters that showed us what happened and what was coming. Then, this same stranger led us through the desert to this place, which we were told would serve as help for a location that was to be prepared for God's people. Then…. He baptized us all and told us to protect the Oasis at all costs. One day, he said we would be delivered upon receiving his mark. So, we wait, like good and experienced soldiers, guarding the most sacred possession to all of Israel. And Maya, when we see a civilian car driven by two women, aimlessly driving towards us, we must stop and vet their intentions like the lives of God's people are at stake." Jessica said, stoically. Maya and Ima were overwhelmed by what Jessica shared. "I understand." Maya said, drawing a sneer from Jessica. "How could you understand?" Jessica asked emotionally, before immediately regaining her composure. "I understand be-cause I was going to school in California when it happened. I was just in town visiting Israel when it went off. I'm the only person I know that escaped from my school. I know your losses. I lost all my friends and my father…" Maya said before stopping abruptly and grabbing her mother's hand. "We lost him. In the incursion. I watch them massacre him, while he protected us. We were still grieving our friends who disappeared when the geyser in Yosemite ignited. I understand it all." Maya pleaded, tearfully. Jessica paused for a moment and stared at Maya. "You saw your father killed by insurgents? My God, I'm sorry. But after seeing them, I trust you understand why we did what we did to you…" She said firmly. "I do." Maya assured, before adding, "I also know the man you're talking about. He's a man who's captivated all of Israel. And if I'm a betting girl, I think he's most likely the same man who told me to come to you with the bag of money. Jessica smiled. "You may win that bet. But the money came from the sons of Israel for us to fuel up one last time. It's inconsequential to what you didn't know was in the bag… What you were meant to bring to us, was under the money. Maya looked dumfounded. "I don't understand. There's only money in there, right?" She asked to Ima. Ima just shrugged. Jessica reached into the bag of money and pulled a small piece of paper from it. "His mark and seal, indicating that you are who we've been waiting for. Maybe he knew you wouldn't come if he gave you just a napkin?" Jessica quipped, as she turned from Maya and made her way down the rest of the stairs, to the group. "Let's eat, all. It's almost time." She said to the team, as they cheered the idea. Maya marveled at the notion of whether she would have come with just the note, as she looked at Ima. Ima nodded. "That's true. I don't think we would have come here with just that dirty napkin." She quipped as she followed Jessica down the stairs.

Chapter 23

As the team filed in, Maya and Ima joined them as each of the team was given a ration case for a meal. Justin brought two cases over to Maya and Ima. "Hopefully there's no hard feelings between us." He said as he offered the food to the women. Ima placed her hand on his shoulder. "You've suffered. I can tell. It's made you untrusting. It's done the same to me." She said, assuredly. Justin nodded, thankful of the gesture as Ima grabbed the two cases from him and brought them over to Maya. Maya watched as the group joined hands. "Will you pray with us?" Justin asked them. Maya nodded and grabbed his hand and took hold of Ima's. "Lord, we give thanks for this meal which is our daily bread. May you're will be done in all things, in the name of your son Jesus Christ, amen.". "Amen" the group exclaimed. Ima smiled towards Maya. "Our first public prayer as Christians." She whispered, excitedly. Maya smiled. She saw Jessica eating by herself in one of the corners, as she looked out at her group. Maya made her way over to her. "Can I sit here?" she asked. Jessica smiled and replied, "It's a free country. Well, sort of.". Maya chuckled. She sat a few feet from where Jessica sat and opened her ration box. "Oh'" she whispered nervously as she looked at the contents. She saw two cans of pre-cooked meat, a can of beans and a packet of apple sauce. "You get used to it." Jessica assured, as she placed a forkful of the pre-cooked gelatin-based meat in her mouth, while jokingly making a choking face. Maya chuckled, as she pulled back the lid from the can and revealed the grey, slimy entrée. She pulled her fork from the case and took a small bite. "How is it?" Jessica asked humorously. "Best can of processed nitrates I've had in years…" Maya said as she cringed at the taste. Jessica laughed as the two ate their meal together. "So, when was the last time you saw him?" Maya asked. "The stranger?" Jessica asked. "Yeah. Mash'pekh. I call him Mash Mash." Maya joked. Jessica looked confused. "I… don't know Mash'pekh." She said. Maya too, looked confused. "It wasn't Mash'pekh that led you here?" she asked, as she took another reluctant bite of the canned meat. "No, his name was Tevah." Jessica replied, garnering more confusion from Maya. "Tevah? I swear the names of these guys…" she joked, as she ate another bite. Jessica chuckled. "Speaking of which…" She said as she stopped eating and looked down to her watch and quickly stood up. "Mike, we've only got an hour. You and Amy get everything ready when you're finished eating." Jessica said. Maya looked down to see the man named Mike nod towards Jessica, before abruptly finishing his food and getting up to do something, followed by a brunette woman. "What's happening?" Maya asked Jessica. "In less than an hour, the Premier will walk out of the temple." She said to Maya, as she placed another forkful of food in her mouth. Maya stopped eating and stared at Jessica, whose eyes were fixed on her food. "What does that mean?" Maya asked. Jessica smiled. "Tevah will be waiting for him outside." Jessica said while chewing, as she grinned towards her food. "What's Tevah going to do?" Maya asked Jessica, as she placed her food on the ground. Jessica swallowed what she was chewing and looked up to Maya. She grinned wickedly. "Vengeance." She said, as she took another bite of her food. Maya froze. She didn't understand what Jessica was implying. Jessica looked and saw Maya's confusion. "Finish your food, Maya." she said, as she continued to eat. "We'll have a front row seat for it all." She added. Maya looked down to see Mike was wheeling in an old television, followed by Amy, who was carrying a small, makeshift satellite of sorts.

Chapter 24

JESSICA AND MAYA WALKED down from the alcove where they were eating and joined the rest of the group. "Everyone accounted for?" Jessica called out as she looked around the room. She nodded to each of her team. "Maya, you've met Justin and Mike. Let me introduce you to everyone else…" she said, before continuing…. "This is Buck, Toni, Phillipe, Bryce, Tyrell, and Amy." Each of the members greeted Maya. Maya smiled at each. "This is my Ima." She said as she pointed to her mother. "Of course, Ima is Hebrew for Mom, so you can call her Esther." She said. Ima protested. "There's not a one here older than thirty years of age yet." She said defiantly to Maya. "They can all call me Ima." She added. The group smiled. Each of them came up to greet Ima and Maya, but none could make it past Ima without being hugged. Jessica came over to Maya. "They needed that, ya know." She said. Maya looked at Jessica confused. "Needed what?" she asked. "They each lost their families. Their mothers and fathers, along with their siblings and friends. Having someone to call *Ima* is a substantial gift for them." Jessica said as she put her arm around Maya and looked at her group relishing in Ima's hugs. Maya smiled warmly. "She had to leave her son Abi, in Jerusalem." He's with Mash'pekh… Our "guy". Our *Tevah*, I guess." She said humorously. "This is as good for her as it is for them. It gives her purpose." Maya added. As the group embraced, Jessica called to Mike. "Are we loaded up?" she asked. Bryce and Mike, both pointed towards the other side of the underground complex. "We are." They assured Jessica. "What's over there?" Maya asked curiously. "We leave here tomorrow." Jessica said. Maya looked at her puzzled. "Where are you going?" Maya asked. "With you and Ima." Jessica responded before looking towards Maya and asking, "Didn't Mash'pekh tell you?". Maya shrugged confusingly. "I feel like I don't know anything right now." She said as she stared at Jessica helplessly. "I get it." Jessica assured her. "When Tevah led us here a year ago, he told us that on the same day he would go to the temple to confront the Premier, two travelers would arrive, and we were to go with them." Jessica said, as her eyes made way to Maya's. Maya stood stunned. "Are you..." Maya began to say while fumbling over her words. "Are you sure it us?" She asked. Jessica giggled. "What are the chances, Maya?" she quipped as she motioned a thumbs up to Mike and Bryce. Maya stood amazed. She looked at Jessica. "So, you're coming with us then?" Maya said excitedly. Jessica smiled and nodded. "Our time here is finished it seems." She said stoically, as she looked around at the darkened underground facility, she and her team had called home, for so long. "When do we leave?" Maya asked. "First light. We'll stop and shore up our fuel with the money. I'm looking it over with Justin and we'll decide where is safest to stop, as soon as Tevah finishes." Jessica responded. "When Tevah finishes? How will we know when that is?" Maya replied. Jessica smiled. "I'll tell you what he told me when I asked that same question...You'll know when the world knows, and it won't be deniable anymore.". Maya stood puzzled, as she struggled to understand Tevah's statement.

Chapter 25

"THREE DAYS, ABI." MASH'PEKH said, as he embraced the young man. Abi didn't fully understand all that was about to happen or why he of all people had been chosen as a witness, but he believed Mash'pekh when he said it was important. He looked over to Tevah and could see the same pep-talk was being given to Tyrus. He watched as Tyrus tearfully embraced Tevah, before taking his famous walking stick. Abi looked back to Mash'pekh. The emotion he saw on the man's face made him realize that this was the moment of greatness that the two had spoken so often about. He couldn't help but feel like Peter, standing with Jesus at the Garden of Gethsemane, having to find faith amid their teacher being imprisoned. As he thought about the unknown fate of Mash'pekh and Tevah, he felt Mash'pekh's hand on his shoulder. "It's time." He said to Abi. Mash'pekh and Tevah laid their belongings down before Abi and Tyrus. They took their dusty, ragged overcoats off to reveal cloaks of sackcloth, that each had been wearing beneath them. Mash'pekh went into his outer ragged garment and began to rummage through it and pulled a clean, sand-colored cloak from the inside. He turned and gave it to Abi and said, "I gave this to someone very special, once. Now, I'm giving it to you. Do well with it, Abi." Abi looked at the cloak and was deeply moved by the gesture and asked, "Are you sure?", his eyes welling with tears at the gift. Mash'pekh nodded as the two embraced once more. Tevah walked towards where both men were standing. He looked at the cloak Abi was holding and smiled, saying, "That's a nice cloak, young man. Take good care of it. And may you receive a double portion of faith when you wear it." Abi smiled and replied, "Thank you Tevah. I will, sir." Tevah smiled and said to the two, "We'll see you soon." Abi and Tyrus nodded, as Abi tucked the cloak into his backpack. They watched as Mash'pekh and Tevah made their way through the opening and into the temple foregrounds.

As Abi watched the two old men make their way through to the temple, he looked over to see that a large assembly of reporters had assembled at the outer gate, with their cameras fixed on the entryway of the temple, where the Premier was expected to exit from his tour. "Wow, look at them all, Tyrus!" Abi marveled as his eyes studied the mass of media coverage. "They'll get plenty of things to see today." Tyrus replied. Abi nodded. He turned and looked at Tyrus and said, "Did they tell you exactly what would happen?" Tyrus shook his head and said, "No. Just that they would confront the Premier and all of Israel would have a chance to see him as he his. I assume they'll be in prison for a long while, after today." Abi thought about what Tyrus had said and said aloud to himself, "What does that have to do with three days?". Tyrus looked at Abi and asked, "What do you mean by that?". Abi replied, "Mash'pekh told me the God of Israel would speak here, in three days from today." I guess, I don't understand how, if they both get arrested." Tyrus shrugged at the statement, before saying, "I have no idea. But could it be that Jesus returns quicker than we thought? Is that possible?" Abi shook his head and replied, "No, that's the mount of Olives. Plus, it's too soon. We still have three years and like seven months, I think. Mash kept saying we're only about in the middle of all of this." Tyrus nodded and said, "Oh, that's right. Tevah said the same. He said - *we were sealed from what's coming.* The wrath of God and whatnot. Though with either of them in prison, it definitely makes me a little nervous." Abi grinned. "Yep, me too. I better just throw it on now then." He said as he reached into his backpack and pulled out the cloak Mash'pekh gave him and put it on. "How's it look?" he asked Tyrus, as he adjusted the cloth over his hooded sweatshirt. "Umm… well… Biblical!" Tyrus exclaimed, before laughingly saying "You definitely have a little

John the Baptist look going on…". The two men did their best to cut the tension of the overwhelming moment, as they watched Tevah and Mash'pekh make their way to where the guards were standing. "Here we go." Abi said to Tyrus as the two men watched nervously.

Chapter 26

GOOD AFTERNOON, I'M JIM Massahn and with me as always is Anna Fredrick. We welcome you all to this very special world broadcast event. We'll be going live to Jerusalem, Israel, where the Premier is expected to address the world after being invited to be among the first to tour Israel's long-awaited, third temple. Again, our team will go live in just a few moments to bring you this broadcast. But first, this breaking news... Darrell Denotheo, the Nobel winning philanthropist and genius mind behind link18, is set to announce the program's newest enhancement, demonstrated earlier this week by the Premier, the infusion of Artificial Intelligence into Link18, and its immediate availability to every chip and chip holder. This exciting enhancement has been exhaustively tested by the greatest scientific minds of our world and the results of this incredible technology have never been available to the human race, until now.

That's right, Jim, this technology was already being dubbed the next great step in the evolution of man, before this new enhancement was announced. Now, having been fully and vigorously tested and approved by the United Nations, once implanted into a body, Link18's neuro detection goes to work as it diagnosis the body for any and all illness. It's designed to treat a myriad of illnesses without medication, however, should something extreme ever be found, the device – having been linked to your digital currency and medical records, orders the appropriate medications to your home. Incredible! The AI component is built to recondition the brain against harmful things like overeating and excessive drinking, while developing healthier habits *of what we eat and how often. The AI component will also treat and even pre-treat the host body for unhealthy thoughts, leading to depression and anxiety, as its suicide prevention measure technology is introduced as a revolution in fighting the surging numbers of those tragically taking their own lives as they fail to cope with such unfortunate, yet treatable illnesses. Jim…*

That's a sobering thought, Anna. The global exchange has seen its first bump in many months at the completion of the temple and the expected announcement of link18 being possibly made free to the world. The current unexpected food crisis and world-wide droughts, combined with continuing global catastrophes have taken their toll on the exchange as continuing fears have mounted. Scientists admit being perplexed by the frequency of these events, despite the successful world-wide effort of reducing carbon, through synthetics. Anna…

Yes, Jim, the synthetics program proved beyond advantageous, as the same technology that was once used to create incredible three-dimensional items through a simple printing process, evolved into a near-zero carbon synthetic food distribution network which now accounts for roughly 90% of the world's food supply. The food, dubbed "Miracle meat" for its incredible meat-like taste and global benefit, has continued to serve families the world over, as everyday items like bread have become harder to supply. Efforts to duplicate Miracle Meat's success with both fruits and vegetables has undertaken some minor setbacks due largely to the recent uptick in the lack of both wind and rain. Scientists, as well as the United Nations, are calling for patience however, as every step and measure is being taken to expedite the rainlink1 program – the second such effort by Mr. Denotheo at creating the much-hyped, synthetic clouds for rain generation. Jim…

Thanks Anna. We now take you live to Jerusalem, where we expect to hear from the Premier.

Chapter 27

TEVAH AND MASH'PEKH MADE their way through the barriers. They walked together between the guarded gates where the reporters were, and the entrance to the temple, completely unbeknownst to the security that was guarding both locations, as if they could not see them. Mash'pekh stopped and turned to face the temple. Tevah walked to the other side of the entryway, and faced the entry gate, where the media was standing. Tevah looked over to Mash'pekh and nodded, saying "For the glory of Yeshua.", which Mash'pekh repeated. Then, Mash'pekh raised his hands in the air. "Lord, now is the time you made known to us." He cried out, startling security and drawing immediate attention from the media that was waiting at the gates. The sky suddenly turned black, as thunder cracked, and lightning flashed. Suddenly, wind began to swirl about the temple grounds. It howled throughout, in a haunting bellow, causing the security detail to be blown off their feet. Those in the media attending, screamed and cried out in fear at the sudden onset. Tevah, still facing the gate where they stood, raised his hands in the sky and cried out. Lightning struck the ground before him. The attendees and the media screamed out in terror at the sight, as their eyes fixed on the two men. In their confusion and fear, some yelled out that the men were insurgents. Others declared it was they who were responsible for the disappearing. Through the calamity, none could look away or stop filming.

Tevah began to walk towards the media, his arms held out wide. "Repent!" he screamed out. His voice thundered throughout the gates and into the entire center of Jerusalem. The media cowered down at the great bellow, yet none stopped filming the incredible event. "Repent, for the kingdom of Christ will return to judge you!" He declared, even louder than before, as his powerful voice seemed to knock over some of the attendees who had withstood the wind. The media attendees froze as none could find the words to report on what they were seeing. As if any power they had to speak had been suddenly seized from them. And yet, none stopped broadcasting. The front entryway guards began to get their bearings. The group of five men helped each other to their feet and did their best to walk through the swirling wind, to where Tevah was speaking. Coming just twenty or so feet away from him, they then drew their weapons at Tevah and ordered him to the ground. Tevah turned to face their direction. He sneered. "The kingdom of the Lord has come upon you this day!" he exclaimed. Immediately, Tevah's eyes turned to fire. The security team, still barely able to stand, was terrified. He cried out with a loud voice, "It is just!" Then, he opened his mouth and recited the beginning of Genesis. As the worlds flowed, they were followed by scorching white flames. The fire poured out from Tevah, as he recited the scripture. It enveloped the men, first surrounding them before violently thrusting itself upon them and incinerating them to their bones. Tevah drew the fire back into his mouth, to reveal the charred remains of the security force.

Chapter 28

THOSE WHO WATCHED, SCREAMED in horror at the sight of what happened. One of the reporters was able to get in front of her rolling camera as she frantically tried to speak… "Something is happening here at the temple. Something is happening! Two intruders are attacking the temple with some sort of weaponry. We don't know who they are or why they're doing this, but they just apparently murdered a helpless security detail for everyone to see." She exclaimed in terror, before adding frantically off-camera… "This could be the ones responsible for the disappearing! Have they come back because of this stupid religious event?"

The second security detail that guarded the entryway, held their positions, and locked their sights on Mash'pekh who was standing about 20 yards away from the entryway. They raised their weapons and attempted to shoot him, but their weapons would not fire. Just as they tried though, Mash'pekh cried out, "It is just!", as he raised his right hand and threw it to the ground. Fire poured from the sky and engulfed the guards, instantly killing them. Those attending watched in horror. Mash'pekh then turned towards them and walked over to where Tevah stood. "Repent!" Mash'pekh cried, his voice thunderously echoing as Tevah's had. "Repent for the kingdom of Christ returns!" he declared as suddenly, the wind once-more howled throughout where the attendees were standing. Like a hurricane of sudden wind, it swept the media once-more from their feet, yet somehow did not upend a single camera. All continued to broadcast the live feed, as the images of the two and their words, swept across the world. Tevah and Mash'pekh each drew their hands out to their sides, as fire returned to their eyes. They looked towards every camera and cried out together.... "Repent of your sins and give yourself over to Christ. Do not take the mark!" As they spoke, their eyes still hauntingly illuminated, hail began to fall across the world. Tevah lifted his leg from the ground and stomped it against the stone. As he did, a great earthquake was felt starting in Israel and reaching its way around the globe. Those in attendance were horrified. "It is them!" some of them cried out, referring to the extraterrestrial beings they held responsible for the disappearing. "It's because they built that darn temple!" some shouted.

As the events continued, several armored, military-style trucks made their way through the barriers. They crashed onto the scene with fury. Abi and Tyrus hid themselves amidst the chaos, still in shock from what they had just witnessed. The trucks emptied, as heavily armed men funneled out and began to open fire on Tevah and Mash'pekh. Yet, no harm could befall the two men. They opened their mouths and shouted aloud, "It is just!". Then, they each began to recite the sermon on the mount, causing fire to pour from their mouths as the scripture was spoken. It consumed the armed men and their trucks, instantly turning all to ash. The driver of another truck, that was set in the distance, did his best to back out through the barriers, but as he attempted to drive around the blazing fire, he and his team were instantly consumed by it as well. The media watched in horror, as the two men unleashed devastation in the center of the temple grounds, on what all expected to be a day of peace.

Chapter 29

MASH'PEKH MADE HIS WAY over to the fiery rubble at the gate's entrance, that was the security team. He placed his hand in the ash heap, grabbing a fistful of the debris. He looked down at the ashes, saddened by the sight. "Lord, be merciful." He whispered as he covered his head with the ashes. Tevah walked towards the burning trucks and placed his hands in the ashes, as well. He looked back at the terrified media, behind him and sneered. "Lord, be just!" he whispered as he covered his head with ashes. The two men returned to their places, on both sides of the temple aisle and began to prophecy, loudly: their voices seemingly carried throughout all of Israel by the wind they summoned and the cameras that continued filming. "Here me, oh Israel!" Tevah bellowed out, as the earth shook. He continued, "Thus says the Lord you're God. Repent, for my judgement comes and none can stand before it. Repent of your false Gods and idols. Repent of your lusts of the flesh. Repent of your lawlessness and wickedness. For the wrath of the Lord comes nigh!" Mash'pekh watched as the media in attendance were frantically trying to cut their live video feeds. "Do not hinder the children of Israel!" he called out to them in a thunderous voice. Every member of the media froze instantly, as each dared not challenge the illuminated eyes that burned towards them. Tevah drew a breath and once more bellowed out raucously, ""Thus says the Lord you're God. Repent, for my judgement comes and none can stand before it. Repent of your false Gods and idols. Repent of your lusts of the flesh. Repent of your lawlessness and wickedness. For the wrath of the Lord comes nigh! This judgement comes upon the whole world. You will not escape the bowls of His wrath. Repent!" As Tevah was speaking, Mash'pekh walked over to the cowering media. Standing just a few feet from their view, his illuminated eyes burned towards them and their cameras. They screamed and covered their faces, from the powerful light he emitted. He stifled the glow and returned his eyes to their normal state. He stared into the cameras, as the still-cowering media began to slowly look up at him. "For 1260 days, we have prophesied. We have struck your lands and skies with the plagues of our Lord. We have caused the skies to not produce your rain. We have stricken the wheat fields and the harvests. We have turned your rivers red. We have unleashed these pangs upon you on behalf of our Lord, Jesus Christ." One of the members of the media, a young man, scowled at the statement. He stood up boldly and challenged Mash'pekh, saying "If that's true, then you're admitting that you murdered billions of good and innocent people for Jesus! Are you kidding? If that's the case, then we reject you and your Jesus, you MURDERERS!" As he declared it, a large piece of hail fell from the sky and struck him, killing him instantly. The other members in attendance, screamed and fell on their faces in horrible fear. Mash'pekh eyes returned to flame. He walked closer to the cameras, garnering screams from the cowering media as they feared his wrath. "I assure you; it is not our wrath you should fear, but the wrath of Him who sent us. You who remain from the caught up, this is you're last warning. Repent! The kingdom of Jesus is near." He said, before turning and regaining his place next to Tevah. As he did, the door to the temple opened.

Chapter 30

"FREEZE!" A VOICE CALLED out from behind the door as the Premier's personal security detail stormed out of the temple, pointing their guns at both Mash'pekh and Tevah. Both men held their hands up in the air. "It is just!" they declared, as the security detail divided into two groups and approached the elder men, to subdue them. Once the detail was divided, standing before both Mash'pekh and Tevah, their eyes instantly illuminated, and their mouths opened with the reciting of Psalm 27:2. And as was such, the words that poured from them, turned once again into fire, and consumed the two groups of the Premier's security detail, reducing them to piles of fallen ash. Screams were heard from the attending media as they watched helplessly. Yet still, the cameras continued to capture everything. The entire world watched in terror as these two men, who had taken full responsibility for the horrible plagues and famine of the world, unleashed their destruction. None could look away.

Most that viewed the disturbing images allowed themselves to be hardened further. They cursed the two men and from the comfort of their homes, they gnashed their teeth at them, as they watched them recite forbidden scripture so boldly and without repercussion. But a small number; a remnant, heard their message and found themselves quietly rejoicing. Their hearts began to rekindle as truth poured through their televisions and radios. The visualization of the events that had just unfolded brought back the memories of forgotten prophecies in the Bible. Their hearts began to echo the ignored and forgotten seeds planted many years ago, by the Christians that once lived before suddenly disappearing. They were reminded of the many social media posts they ignored and the family members they severed ties with over this same message. Their hearts were made to recall the many times they turned ministry away, in favor of the life that the world offered. And yet now, this same message; the now-forbidden message of Jesus Christ, was being cast on every screen throughout the world, unimpeded. And though many scoffed, those who did not were given wisdom and a thirst. As those hearts were searched, the ears that chose to finally hear, a cry was made by Tevah… "Seal them, Lord!"

The ground shook, violently as the onlookers once more screamed out in terror. Lightning flashed across the darkened sky, as thunder cracked loudly over the entire globe. Mash'pekh and Tevah raised their hands towards heaven and praised the God of Israel for His mercy; their eyes welled with tears, no longer showing the fire of the Holy Spirit. "Thank you, Lord our God for the gift you have given to your children. Their hearts have been rekindled and their heads are sealed. Give them strength to endure what comes and to continue our work until all is fulfilled." They said, in unison. Abi and Tyrus, overwhelmed by the display, watched as the two men took their former places on each side of the entryway to the temple. Mash'pekh turned his head slightly towards Abi and winked, before returning his gaze towards the temple. A rush of calm, like a warm breeze, rushed over Abi as peace overtook him. The two elderly men who had caused such devastation and havoc in the name of Jesus Christ, watched the front of the temple, and waited patiently: neither looking away from the opened door. As they watched, their eyes fixed, a figure in the distance emerged. It was the Premier.

Chapter 31

"THE PREMIER!" A VOICE called out, from behind where the two men were standing, as the media began to rise to their feet and cheer at his appearing. "Now they're in trouble!" another onlooker yelled, as the crowd grew bold in their opposition of the two strangers. He stepped forward from the doorway of the temple and walked to the banister that overlooked the courtyard, where Tevah and Mash Pek stood quietly on each side of the entryway path. The Premier smiled at the men and gently shook his head to them. He then slowly walked down the steps towards where they stood, until he was standing directly on the pathway that divided them, just a few yards away. He looked around at the destruction and continued to shake his head. As his eyes took in all the two had done, he looked up to both men and smiled, as the crowds behind the media began to pour in to watch. He stood before them stoically, cleared his throat and spoke loudly and in ear shot of the media and their cameras…. "I remember the stories I was told as a child. Bible stories. Stories meant to be a light, but too filled with darkness to illuminate the intelligent person's heart. Stories filled with hurt and torment. Stories of murder, theft, and rape. Stories of Prophets and mystical men that could fool an entire world with their words and their ways. And so blindly these sheep follow them, never to ask the necessary questions; where are we being led to and why? I remember those days in my childhood hearing about the days of the lying prophets and their damage to our world. But gentlemen, those days are simply no more." The crowd that had gathered at the media gate erupted at the words the Premier spoke to the two men, who stood silently, almost reverently before him. The Premier put his hands up to calm the watching crowd; their eyes fawning over his every move. As he did, he was joined by Darrell Denotheo, who stood behind the Premier and watched from the staircase just outside the temple doorway. The Premier then confidently started walking down the entryway, and between Tevah and Mash'pekh, as both stood quietly. The media once more roared, at the Premier's show of boldness. Abi watched nervously, as neither of the elderly men moved from their now somber gaze. They just stood still, as the Premier brazenly walked between them, towards the media. "Get him, guys." He heard Tyrus whisper, impatiently. But neither man budged. The Premier then stood the same distance from the still-rolling cameras, as Mash'pekh had, a few minutes before. "I'm going to prove something to you all today." The Premier stated with boldness. The media relished the charismatic man's words as they stood eager to hear them. He continued…. "You now see who is responsible for the disappearing, as well as the last three years of catastrophic events. They've admitted such and the world has noted their confession. And if that were not enough, the lie of religion that we've worked so hard to eliminate, that has done so much harm to our world, is the same lie these two murderers have spoken. All authority has been offered to me by the United Nations, to lead us from this deception and protect us from anyone who seeks to take the world we've built together." He said, stoically to thunderous applause, before continuing…. "Shall I use this authority on these two? Shall I demonstrate the power of man against the so-called power of Heaven for you?' he cried as he raised his hands upward and shook his fist to the sky. The crowd erupted in cheers as they began to chant, "Kill them. Kill them all. Kill them. Great and small." The Premier turned towards Tevah and Mash'pekh and smiled, as he walked once more between the two, as each remained silent. "The people have spoken, gentlemen.' He said playfully as he passed them, before walking up to where Mr. Denotheo was standing. The two men stood together, as they faced Mash'pekh and Tevah, whose eyes raised up to where they stood.

As they watched the Premier lift his hands in the sky, the veil lowered before them to reveal Satan, in all his fallen glory, standing beside the Premier, controlling his speech, as he spoke. Both men could then see clearly, Azul standing beside Darrell Denotheo, as he manipulated his every move and thought. As words poured from the premier, Tevah and Mash'pekh were suddenly overcome by the unclean spirits that were at work in the men. They each raised their heads towards heaven. As the Premiers hands were raised, a drone controlled by each of his hands came to the sides of both men, as the crowd's chanting grew louder and louder. Abi and Tyrus watched helplessly. "What are they doing?" Tyrus asked in fear as he watched the drones come within a few feet of both men. Abi's peace however was doubled as was his faith. "It is written." The spirit whispered out from his lips to the ears of Tyrus, who also received a sudden and immediate peace. They watched as the Premier grinned wickedly; with chants of "Kill them. Kill them all. Kill them. Great and small." Echoing out throughout all of Israel. Then, the Premier threw both of his hands to the ground, with a mighty thrust. A sudden burst of light shot forward from each of the drones, severing the heads of both Tevah and Mash'pekh, killing them instantly.

Chapter 32

As THE LAST OF the equipment was loaded, none of Jessica's team said a word. Each kept to themselves as their minds attempted to process the events they witnessed. Maya, heavy hearted after witnessing the brutal death of her friend Mash'pekh, sat quietly in the armored truck the soldiers were loading. Her heart was heavy for the loss of her friend. She remembered what Mash'pekh told her, about the spiritual battle that was being waged for Israel and how she and Abi had each been chosen to witness. Still, the reality that had gripped Maya over the last week; one that took the normalcy of her life and shook it to dust, was fully setting in. She wiped her tears and sniffed. "Help me, Lord." she whispered out before standing up to go and find Ima. As she stepped out of the truck, she scanned the emptied underground fortress and saw the team was ready to make the trip to Petra. She saw Justin calling the group together but didn't see Ima and Jessica. She made her way swiftly up the staircase and saw Ima helping Jessica with the shaft pin, that locked the steel entry door to the facility. "That's it. We got it." Jessica said as she high-fived Ima. Both women then turned to see Maya standing behind them, looking somber. Ima walked up to her daughter and put her arms around her and asked, "I didn't want to disturb you. Are you ok?". Maya nodded. She looked over to Jessica, who was still sealing the door's access point. "Give me a minute Mom." Maya said, as Ima nodded before making her way to their staircase. Maya walked over to Jessica and watched as she filled each of the crevices of the door with foam. "What's that do?"

Maya asked curiously. "It makes it a perfect conduit for the explosives we installed." She replied, before finishing and looking up at Maya. "You, ok?" she asked. Maya nodded. "I'm still processing. Question is... How are you?" Maya replied, before adding.... "You seem somewhat unscathed.". Jessica smiled and stood up. "How many soldiers have you led?" She asked. Maya shrugged at the question. "Ok, I'll take that as none. So, this makes my next question even easier for you to answer... How many soldiers under your command have you lost?" Maya just stared at Jessica. There was no way she could respond. She watched Jessica, the petite and feisty blonde soldier with her rugged bravado, as she rummaged into her vest. She pulled a necklace from it that was tucked under her shirt. She raised the necklace to reveal a slew of dog tags attached; each from a fallen member of her team, and far too numerous to count. Jessica stared at Maya and shook the necklace loudly, before placing it back beneath her vest. She said, "When you've seen as much death as I've seen, you tend not need as much time to grieve. Don't get me wrong, Maya, if you want to grieve and go into an existential crisis, that's fine. I have no problem with that. But while you are being afforded that time to do so, my team and I are finishing everything Tevah told us to do before leaving here. Some of us have been refined by death to not let it blow us off course, no matter how painful it is to see." Jessica's eyes gave Maya a glimpse of the pain she carried under her tough and hardened exterior. Maya was humbled by what Jessica had said. The more she learned about the woman the more she found herself identifying with her. She walked over to her, paused before her, and quickly placed her arms around her. Jessica at first, was reluctant to respond. She held her arms to her sides, as Maya embraced her. But after a few seconds, Maya felt Jessica hold on to her, as the two embraced. "I'm sorry." Maya whispered, bringing a sudden thaw to the hardened exterior of Jessica. The two embraced quietly, away from the others, as the weight of everything they had encountered could no longer be ignored. They then returned to the loaded truck and took their seat, as the team set off together on their mission to Petra.

Chapter 33

As the men filed into his camp, Ashem could see the somberness that was sweeping the men. He saw Dante coming in with his group, his eyes red from his tears. He embraced him. "Hello old friend.". Dante hugged Ashem with an air of defeat in his spirit. "I just can't believe he's gone." Dante said tearfully. Ashem nodded and hugged the man once more. "Not gone." He responded assuredly as he pointed his finger towards Heaven. Dante nodded. Just then, Tomas came up to both and embraced Ashem. He too had been crying as the men who had hiked the entire day together from his camp, listened on their radios in horror, as the events unfolded. With Tomas, was Siff and Danny. "Men, have you eaten?" Ashem asked to the four. "I don't think any of us can right now." Danny replied somberly. Ashem nodded. "Let's get fires started and everyone in a rested state. We'll be leaving at the third hour, for Petra. Spread the word to each of the group leaders, we'll be doing a reading together in two hours. This is not to be missed. The spirit comes with the seal and this message is from the spirit." He said as each of the exhausted men nodded. They put the message out as the massive camp of men did their best to find comfort in the foothills of the mountains; each overwhelmed by the loss of the two patriarchs of their calling.

Ashem knew the weight each was carrying that night, as he walked through the crowd, greeting each of the thousands of men who had arrived. He was the only one Tevah had confided in, about his would-be death at the hands of the Premier. He knew he was one of only two men that had been given a message of hope to give to those defeated by the two men's deaths; that in just three and a half days after their death, the God of Israel would make his appeal. Ashem believed with conviction, Tevah's words. He held his Bible tight as he walked through the camp and saw the saddened and defeated faces, knowing that Tevah had given him a scripture that would heal every broken heart that night. All each somber man had to do, was muster enough faith to go out from their sadness and fear, and hear the words he would read aloud, in unison with the group leaders. Like the serpent in the wilderness, this simple act of faith was where the group's healing would be found. It was the group's second test apart from Tevah; the first being the Apostolic march that saw each of them carry the good news of Jesus, to the doorsteps of all of Israel over the last year.

Ashem made his way over to Tomas as the two had made their camp together at the end of the mountain's ridge, apart from the others. "Everyone's accounted for but two, Ashem." Tomas said, curiously. Ashem nodded. Tomas was confused and asked, "Where are the other two we're missing?" Ashem smiled and replied, "Ground zero." Tomas just stared at Ashem, curious of how he could be smiling at such a time. "What has that smile on you're face, brother?" Tomas asked, eagerly. Ashem pulled his Bible from under his arm and cleared his throat and said, "Tonight's scripture, which Tevah told me I would be reading after this night." Tomas stood up quickly. "What is it that would have you smiling to yourself right now?" he said demandingly. "Tonight, we'll be reading Revelation 11:11." Ashem responded, as he turned towards the encampment and gazed at Tevah's vision coming true.

Chapter 34

GOOD EVENING, I'M JIM Massahn and welcome to world news. It's been just under 48 hours since the religious extremists attacked the temple and were thwarted by none other than the Premier himself, using the same technology that saved his life just a few years ago. What a story, as we go live to Anne who is boots on the ground at the temple. Hello Anne and Happy Deliverance Day to you!

Happy Deliverance Day to you, Jim! That's the theme here at the new temple, where the bodies of the two intruders have not been removed, but are still viewable to the public, on orders from the Premier. People are gathering here at ground zero, where the invaders that had tormented the planet for so long, were stopped by the Premier himself. The Premier has since stated that not only has his team uncovered the origin planet of the invaders, but that his office has in fact found a way to intercept communication from them, using technology from link18. It was during this interception that the horrifying truth of our planet, was revealed. It appears that for thousands of years, Earth and her resources have been the envy of other worlds. To preserve the planet from a war that would consume her resources, it appears that religion was given to us as a means to destroy each other through mindless obedience that would destroy the human race, leaving most of our planet unharmed, unspoiled, and uninhabited. Mr. Denotheo has submitted irrefutable evidence to the United Nations that those who were waiting to invade our planet, those responsible for the disappearing, have left our atmosphere after the events that unfolded yesterday. Because of the deterrence, the *bodies will lie in the square for all to see as a message to all that this world and its culture will not be bow down to anyone beyond our clouds. The United Nations, in response to the evidence, declared this day to be recognized by the world as "Deliverance Day; the day all of Earth was freed from the shackles of the lie. Jim...*

Thank you, Anne and I think I speak for most when I say the Premier's speech gave me chills. Like a superhero written about in comics or folklore, Earth now has a powerful protector and deterrent. We have certainly turned an evolutionary corner as a race; no longer shackled by the fabrication of foreign beliefs and the horrific power of manipulation associated with faith in a deity. This is a liberating day for all and as was made known earlier today in the same speech, Link18 will now not just be available to all free of charge, but in order to live socially in this brave new world, it is the only way to do so. We go live to foreign correspondent Getty Haynes for more.... Getty?

That's right Jim. In a bold and assertive declaration, the Premier has convinced the UN to make link18 the standard passport for all economic and social participation. After such a demonstration of the technology's ability as a global deterrent, there's simply no argument that can be levied against such thinking. Now that we know, scientifically that Religion was a weapon used to destroy us from the inside through manipulation, the calls to unite and oust any former allegiances to those archaic beliefs have been answered through the availability and mandatory implantation, of link18. As of today, link18 in all her glory, will be made available to the world free of any charge. Back to you, Jim...

Thank you, Getty. That is tremendous breaking news, Getty thank you. The United Nations has acted, and I think the world over is ready for such bold new action. We're going live now to the Premier as he and his team exit the general assembly of the UN to share with us all, what's next.

"Ladies and gentlemen thank you for being here to witness this historic occasion in our world history. The power of man and woman is the truth in their heart. The human heart has been cast horribly throughout history. Today, we end that myth. The power of

our enemies, is in their heads, as demonstrated by how they were defeated. As a global society, it is incumbent on us all to now understand that any abstaining or resistance to link18, will result in exposing the entire population to the long-planned annihilation, by foreign invaders. I fully concur that the safety of the many will now absolutely outweigh the stubbornness of the few. We must now move forward with a world directive that all must abide by for the peace and safety of our world. In order to take part in this brave new society, you must simply receive link18. Faith-based demonstrations, in the wake of such overwhelming evidence of its danger to our world, will be met swiftly, as it was with the two invaders. What that means, is any refusal of link18 or any continuing statements of faith, will be met as acts of treason by a foreign invading force and punishable by the only means we know that stops them…. The removal of their heads. That is why we are leaving the invaders bodies lying in view. To deter our enemies from any further attacks and to deter skeptics and conspiracy theorists that this was anything but a planned attack. There is only one way forward. We can no longer be conservative in our thinking and way of life. We must unite as we did after the disappearing. We must unite as a people, unequivocally accepting of things like each other's race, or sexual preferences. We must unite as a people determined not to let any agents of foreign malice, harm us again. I can provide no greater evidence of the why. Their bodies are still there for all to see."

There we have it, friends. It's a joyous day. A historic day. A critical day. The Premier has given this world the clear path and only way forward. And for many, myself included, we've waited far too long for it. From all of us here at world news, good night.

Chapter 35

"*ABI...*" ABI HEARD HIS name called and woke suddenly from his sleep, looking up at the strange ceiling. He then slowly turned and stared into the darkness. He gazed around the poorly lit room, doing his best to see. As he scanned the room he didn't recognize, he remembered he was staying at Tyrus's apartment. He exhaled. "Still jumpy." He exclaimed. He closed his eyes once more to try and rest. "*ABI...*" he heard a voice call out. He opened his eyes and jumped from the couch he was sleeping on. "Tyrus?" he nervously called out to the darkness. But no answer. As he looked around, he saw an illumination coming from the front window, that overlooked the main square. He walked carefully through the dark room, over the window. He scanned the outside and was surprised to find a now-sleeping city that just a few hours earlier, had been overrun by famous politicians, celebrity visitors and raucous celebrations all their to celebrate the world's new lie... Deliverance Day. Abi looked out the window towards the temple that stood off in the distance. He gazed out somberly as he recalled the events that transpired. Then, he shook his head and turned coldly from the window, to go back to bed. "Abbi!!!" A voice called out, much louder than before. Abbi was startled immediately and turned quickly to the window to see two illuminated pillars were shining bright in the distance. His eyes widened as he turned to find his clothes. As he wrestled in the darkness to find his scattered clothing and backpack, he dressed himself and ran out of Tyrus's building, making a speedy dash to the temple. As he ran through the streets towards the temple, he saw that there was no one out that evening. "Where is everyone?" he thought to himself, as he recalled the masses he had seen out celebrating before going to sleep. As he ran ahead, his eyes suddenly caught movement, coming from the sides of the roads. He looked around and could see shadowy, evil-looking figures emerging from all around him. Their eyes burned bright when they saw Abi running in the middle of the road. Abi was terrified, yet still, he ran as fast as his legs could carry him, desperate to get to the source of light coming from the temple. The shadows howled at him and cursed him, as he ran. They funneled behind him and began to give chase. Abi refused to look back towards them, fearing he would lose his footing, but as he ran, he heard their numbers growing behind them. He saw the horrific things all standing or hovering along every home and building, hanging from random signs and streetlights. As the temple came to view, Abi, near winded, did his best to accelerate. He could see the temple stood unguarded and was empty. Suddenly, the sound from behind him erupted, like a waterfall – as if there were thousands of the creatures, chasing just footsteps behind him. Abi screamed out in fear, as he was just a few feet from the temple. Then, he felt a tug on his backpack, from behind. Abi screamed in terror as he felt himself lose balance. He fell face first to the ground just at the temple's entrance, tumbling hard. While on the ground, he heard them pouring in behind him, just a few feet from where he had tripped, as if they were toying with him. He turned himself over and saw the terror up close. Hovering before Abi were thousands of the horrific creatures, all gazing wickedly at him. Suddenly, they drew sharp dagger-like objects from their bodies, that oozed liquid from their sharpened black tips. Abi looked helplessly in terror as the swarm burst towards him in a screaming rage. They poured over Abi, each thrusting their razor-sharp spikes at him, without pause or mercy. Abi screamed from the pile, as they overcame him.

Chapter 36

THE SWARM RAISED OFF Abi, to reveal him cowering from their attack. Abi laid in place, screaming still, as they raised themselves higher into the air. Noticing he was no longer under their attack, he reluctantly looked up to see them flying into a strait formation, before funneling into a crack in the ground before him. Abi sat up and did his best to catch his breath. He was overwhelmed and confused by what just happened. He looked around at the dimly illuminated city, to see it was still so oddly quiet, with nobody out. He picked himself up from the ground, turned and walked carefully into the unguarded temple grounds entryway. There he saw two glowing figures, their light illuminating all the way to the clouds, as they stood standing where the bodies of Mash'pekh and Tevah were still lying. Abi froze in their presence and fell with his face to the ground before them, overcome by fear. He suddenly felt a hand on his trembling shoulder. "Abi…" he heard a voice again call out. It was the same voice that called him from the apartment. He reluctantly looked up to see the glowing figure of a young man smiling at him. Abi stared in amazement at the person, whose skin seemed like lightning and whose robe was brighter than the sun. As he stared though, the young man's face took sudden shape to resemble Mash'pekh. Abi immediately got up and put his arms around Mash'pekh, as Mash'pekh too, embraced the young man. As he hugged him, Abi saw the other illuminated person, another young and powerful looking man, moving towards them. As he watched him, the second person became clear to Abi, as Tevah was revealed. Abi put his hand out to him, as he continued to embrace Mash'pekh. Tevah grabbed Abi's hand and embraced him. Abi looked at the two still-illuminating men and marveled. "What is this?" he asked them. Mash'pekh smiled. "Who we truly are, in Christ."

Abi marveled as he just stared at the glory of the once-frail looking old men. Their youth and power had been restored and they now towered over Abi. Their glow radiated throughout the temple grounds and into the city. He then began to weep bitterly at the realization that he watched the two men be killed. Mash'pekh again, embraced him. After a few minutes of comfort in each other's presence, Abi regained his composure. "Am I dreaming?" he asked as he again looked around at the quiet city around them. Tevah nodded, before saying in a new, thunderous voice… "You are dreaming, but believe we are here. On the third day at the mid-point, you must return to this temple and prophesy, clothed in the cloak you were given." Abi nodded in wonder. Then he started to remember how many people there were at the temple, since the two men's deaths. Then, Abi recalled seeing the powerful military arm of the Premier was there. He became nervous at the thought. "How can I possibly do this? What would I even say?" He asked fearfully. "The Lord is with you *both*. You will know when you wake. Because the Lord your God is with you, *they* are subject to you." Mash'pekh said, his voice sounding like a rushing river. Abi stared at the men. "Who are *they*?" he asked, nervously. Tevah and Mash'pekh looked at Abi. The men began to lift from the ground as they returned to the clouds. Abi stood confused. He screamed out, "Who are *they*?" as Mash'pekh and Tevah disappeared into the sky. Abi watched the sky for a moment, before turning away. He wondered who the "*they*" were. As he thought deeply, he found himself standing where he fell earlier and was attacked by those horrifying creatures. He looked around at the eerily quiet and empty streets, just outside of the temple gates. Knowing he was dreaming, he looked up to the sky and screamed as loud as he could… "Who are *they*?" He watched the night sky in hope of a response, but none was offered. He stepped off the curb where he had fallen earlier and as he walked back towards Tyrus's apartment, a massive gale swept through the city and the streets. It howled violently. Abi braced himself as best he could, as the wind pushed against the temple walls, behind where he was standing. Then, from the wind, a voice called out to Abi… "The first woe."

Chapter 37

Abi awoke instantly and gasped as he raised himself fearfully off the couch. He looked around the room to see it bright, as the sun poured through the windows. He recognized it was Tyrus's apartment. He ran to the window to see there was huge gatherings still happening in the streets. He squinted his eyes out to see the temple, where he saw people in the distance, still coming together and celebrating. He exhaled in relief and turned from the window, making his way to back to the couch and sat down, putting his head into his hands. Just as he did, he was startled by a voice calling out from the hallway…. "Dude…". He looked up to see a visibly shaken Tyrus, his hair tossed about, slowly emerging from his bedroom. Abi watched as Tyrus walked slowly over to the couch, before slumping down beside him; his eyes fixed on Abi's Bible. "You, ok?" Abi asked him. Tyrus sat quietly for a few seconds, before exhaling. He then looked at Abi, and said… "The first woe…". Abi's eyes widened in shock.

As the two young men discussed what each had seen in their dreams that night, both marveled at the similarities. It was clear that each had truly seen Mash'pekh and Tevah in their restored glory, but it wasn't immediately clear why. Tyrus described the same creatures in his dream but shared he was also spoken to by an Angel who told him at the commencement of the glory, to strike the ground seven times with Tevah's makeshift cane after Abi prophesied, and help would come. Abi looked confused and asked, "Did he say who *they* were. The help?" Tyrus shook his head and replied, "I asked. I screamed it, but no response." Abi smiled, knowing he did the same in his dream. They marveled as each went back and forth over what they had seen and what it could mean. As they debated their visions throughout the early and latter parts of the morning, Abi's watch alarm started to sound. He sat somberly. "Exactly three days to the moment." He said aloud as he looked at his watch. Tyrus looked at him puzzled, and asked "What do you think was so significant about the *three days*?" Abi shrugged and replied "I don't know. We did what we were told though and spread the message. Everyone's going to be watching today, so whatever happens, it will be to God's glory." Just as he finished speaking, a sudden rush of wind swept through the apartment as it gusted like it had in Abi's dream. Tyrus and Abi were startled as papers and debris flew throughout the entire living area, at the force from the powerful gusts. "Whoa, who left the windows opened!" Tyrus yelled out, as he made his way over to close them. But as he did, he saw they were all closed. He looked fearfully back to Abi, who was clutching the couch, to try and brace himself. Suddenly, two small flickering flames seemed to illuminate on the ceiling of the apartment, as the wind continued to swirl. They watched bewilderingly, as each of the two flames molded into the shape of a fiery tongue, before resting over the head of each of them. Their eyes widened as the flames rested on each of their foreheads, as neither was harmed. The wind came to a stop, almost immediately as the two men looked at each other, their eyes still widened. Abi attempted to speak... But was startled to hear himself suddenly speaking in French. He tried again and his words came out in Russian. He looked at Tyrus, in shock at what was happening. Tyrus tried to speak and at first, his words poured out in effortless Cantonese. He tried once more but was dumfounded when he heard himself speaking flawlessly in Japanese. Both men stood in silent awe.

Chapter 38

IN THE DISTANCE, ASHEM looked over the sandy dunes, towards the mountains. It was the sixth hour of their march, and the sun began to blare down on the massive group. "Over the hill and through that ridge?" Sif asked as each of the leading men began to struggle. Ashem, doing his best to stay composed for the sake of the group, nodded, as he too began to break from the heat. "Let no man take his mind from the scripture we heard. If God's will can produce that, surely, we can once more make it through a desert!" He cried out to the leaders, as he marched forward bravely, through the once water-filled pathway. The leaders turned and walked into the crowds behind them, echoing loudly, the words of Ashem, until they made their way throughout the thousands of young men, marching behind them. The deep embankment was filled with their echo as they together, marched towards the place that was to be prepared. As the words were recited, echoes began to ring deep within the group. Suddenly, the echoes turned to calamity, as the sound of their chanting was turned to worry and concern. Ashem came to a sudden stop and turned to look back at the massive number of young men. He squinted to see in the distance, dust being swirled up from afar as a speeding metal object appeared to gleam in the distance. "What is that?" a panicked Danny, rushed to ask as he and the others looked out. Tomas took binoculars out of his sack and looked, before handing them to Ashem. "It's OWL." He said nervously, before adding, "See for yourself.", as he handed Ashem the binoculars. Ashem looked carefully, as the men began to dispute what to do. "We need to fight them!" Siff declared to the others as Danny agreed. "We can't!" Tomas demanded, emphasizing the exhaustion of the men in the group. "We haven't a single weapon among the thousands here!" he added. The thousands in tow began to move quicker up to where Ashem was standing, as he looked out towards the oncoming vehicle. "Wait!" he screamed out, his voice echoing into the entire cavern and thundering out to the entire group. He held up his hand to them telling them to stop, as they all watched helplessly. He turned to Tomas, smiled, and said, "There's only one truck. It's them." Tomas looked through the binoculars to see Ashem was right. A single heavy-armor KrAZ-6322 barreled towards them, with a white banner being waved from the passenger window. "It's them!" Tomas screamed aloud as the leaders of the groups repeated his exclamation throughout the attendees, as it was met with thunderous applause. The truck drove alongside the massive group, beeping its horn repeatedly, as they made their way to the front where Ashem was leading. As the truck pulled up to where Ashem and the other leaders were standing, a small head emerged from the passenger window, with a voice yelling out… "Do you boys need a ride?" The door opened to reveal a fatigue-clad woman. She jumped down form the truck. "Bout time you got here, Jess!" Ashem said as he walked up to Jessica and hugged her. "Is it ready?" he asked eagerly, his eyes glancing over the well-supplied truck from front to back. Jessica smiled and replied, "You'll see. We've been busy." Ashem smiled and asked, "How is everyone holding up?". Jessica sighed. "It was a long trip. Not as long as yours though, I guess." She quipped. Ashem chuckled and said, "Let's get this thing to Petra and get to work." Jessica nodded. She waved to the thousands around them as she and her team drove ahead to the ruins of Petra, where they were to stay and wait for the remnant God would call to them.

Chapter 39

AS THEY UNLOADED THE truck, Maya stepped out from its back and looked around at the massive compound. "I've never seen this part of her before." She exclaimed to Ima who stepped off the truck, behind her. "Tourists don't get to come this way, I suppose. I still can't believe part of the river out there dried up." Ima replied, marveling as she took in the structures and their beauty. Maya nodded and smiled warmly and said, "Sounds like something Mash'pekh and Tevah did...". Ima chuckled. "We'll load everything into the deep recesses." Mike said aloud to Jessica, as he walked past Maya, breaking her an Ima's focus away from the sights. Both women turned and helped Jessica and her team as they unloaded food, water, and munitions from the truck. As Maya was unloading, she looked over everything that was packed. "Is that supposed to feed all of those people we passed?" She quietly asked Ima, who just shrugged. Maya and Ima followed Mike and Phillipe as each carried their boxes of supplies through a narrow rock-based corridor. Maya looked at Ima and smirked. "These guys and their tunnels..." She joked. As she said it, a sudden bright light shined across her face, as the tunnel opened to a massive underground room, filled with hundreds of deep caves. Maya and Ima were stunned by the site. "Wow!" they both exclaimed, garnering laughter from Mike and Phillipe as they brought their packages to a vacant catacomb in the lower rocks, before placing it inside. Mike walked over to Maya and stood beside her. "What do you think we've doing the last two years?" he said with a chuckle, referring to the thousands of stored boxes of supplies. Maya could see containers of food and water, enough to last for years, all meticulously tucked away by Jessica and her team over time. She marveled at the sight, realizing how long all of it must have taken Jessica and her team. Despite all their personal hardships and losses, being thousands of miles from their homes and being under the threat of constant danger, Maya was amazed at how they selflessly dedicated themselves to fortifying Petra; a hidden landmark once considered a wonder to the world but forgotten and made vacant after the disappearing and droughts. Jessica and her team didn't do it for themselves, their families, or their friends. They did it for the children of Israel. Maya stood in amazement of the revelation.

She immediately went out from the tunnel into where she knew Jessica and the rest of her team were still unloading. She found Jessica greeting Ashem, who had just arrived with the massive group, from their trek through the valley. Thousands of men began to pour into the compound. Ashem, though exhausted, was directing the men to go into the furthest chamber of Petra where Jessica and her team had repaired and reassembled the aqueduct, giving the men clean water and refreshment. The men all sang praises when they came to the fountain area, as the entire quarters became filled with their harmonious melody. Jessica watched joyfully, as the men graciously thanked her and her team. She smiled at the accomplishment of their immense work together. Just as she was taking it in, Maya came up to her and stood by her side. Jessica pretended to ignore her. Maya stood next to her for a moment and then gently nudged Jessica's arm, playfully. "I know you probably don't take compliments well, but... Wow." she whispered as she joined her new friend in looking at what was accomplished. Jessica smiled and nudged her back. Both women stood together taking in the cavern's completion and the arrival of the first of many. Then, Justin called out to Jessica from one of the tunnels… "We're all set in here!". Jessica, ever so focused, immediately snapped from her gaze and walked towards one of the tunnels. Maya, confused, followed her, calling out…. "What's up now?" Jessica waved Maya to follow her, saying "We must get the feed running. We're just a few hours away from being at the three-and-a-half-day mark."

Chapter 40

CONFUSED BY THE SIGNIFICANCE, Maya followed behind Jessica, as they walked into a different clearing, which opened to an even larger catacomb. "Whoa!" Maya exclaimed at the vast size of the cavern, as her voice echoed throughout. Jessica smiled, pointing Maya's attention behind her, and said, "I know. It's a little overwhelming. This is where we'll set up our satellites so we can have a live feed for the men to see." Maya, still studying the cave, turned, and looked to see Jessica pointing towards a breathtakingly massive flat stone wall, on the other side of the cave. The wall, an enormous fixture of dull white granite, was a different hue from the red rocks of Petra and stood out boldly. Suddenly, a flicker of light hit the center of the rock. Maya looked up at the source of the flicker and could see projection lights coming from where Bryce and Amy were standing, in an adjacent cave about 40 feet up from where she and Jessica stood. She turned to see the light was a video feed of the world news. "Do we have audio yet?" Jessica called out. Amy gave her a thumbs up, indicating their audio was working. Jessica whispered to Maya and asked playfully, "Want to see something cool?" She and Maya ventured into one of the catacombs, where a massive throw-switch was located. The throw-switch looked to be newer, having been installed recently in the rock and fastened to wires that now ran throughout the caves. Jessica walked over to it and put two hands underneath, before looking back towards Maya and smiling, saying "Ready?". Maya watched as Jessica then placed her petite frame under the switch and hoisted it upwards, giving way to a jolting noise coming from inside the rocks. Suddenly, the caverns illuminated at once, giving way to faint white lights, throughout. "No way!" Maya exclaimed, marveling at the sight of the beautiful illumination, against the reddened haze of the rocks. Jessica stood back with Maya as the two continued to look around. "That's the great thing about deserts. There's plenty of sunlight to run these solar power generators we've been installing here the last two years." She said, as Maya just marveled. "It reminds me of Christmas time in America." Maya marveled. Jessica smiled at the warm memories. Then, Jessica and Maya made their way back to the massive room to see the large granite rock was now showing a clearer picture of the world news broadcast. "Where's the audio?" Maya said to Jessica as she looked up at the rock. "I have to warn the boys first before we turn that on, so they know it's just a news-cast and not OWL. Otherwise, we'll have 143,998 panicked resi-dents to try and calm." She joked, as Toni and Tyrell brought her a wired intercom and a bottle of water. Jessica grabbed the water. "Ooh, thank you guys, I'm definitely parched." Jessica said as she took a gulp. She then handed the bottle to Maya who also took a big sip. Jessica then cleared her throat and announced within the cave, "Attention everyone, as you can see, we have power. I repeat we have power. In an hour's time we'll be asking everyone to make their way to the main cavern where the great stone is. I repeat, in an hour's time, please make your way carefully to the main cavern where the great stone is." Jessica then looked around at everything, as her team, Maya, and Ima, assembled next to her, proudly taking in two years of work. She turned and smiled at the group. "Not bad, everyone. Not bad at all." She said magnanimously. As they took in their accomplishment, Justin brought boxes of rations to each of them. Jessica smiled to Justin and turned to Maya and Ima, saying playfully... "I think we've earned a meal, what do you think guys?" Maya smiled and grabbed two of the rations' boxes from Justin. The group prayed, as was their custom and then sat down together to enjoy their well-deserved meal, spending their free hour of time together, before the room they were in would be filled with thousands of men eager to watch the live broadcast of the Premier, at the temple. As they ate, they reminisced on all they had endured to get to this point.

Chapter 41

ABI FASTENED HIS CLOAK, tightly, under his hooded jacket. As he and Tyrus walked towards the gate of the temple, they could see thousands of people cheering and celebrating the third day of *Deliverance Day*. The two men watched as people were exchanging wrapped gifts with each other. Some were singing songs together, while others had moved on to more blatant and obscene gestures. Many men and women alike were naked, marching in front of the temple, their bodies painted with bloody letters in rejoice of their "Deliverance". There were acts of lewdness and public fornication shamelessly on display, as the two men walked boldly and determined, through the sickened crowd. As they made their way through them, the sin became more and more wretched, the closer they got to the temple ground's front entry gate. Both men noticed that all in attendance were proudly displaying link18's logo on their foreheads. The two were grieved at the sight, knowing full well what the implications were for those who took the mark. As they walked to the front of the temple gate, where both men had dreamed about the night before, they turned and faced the crowd, seeing all the sin firsthand. Both wept at the sight of the once beloved and faithful town that now resembled how Sodom and Gomorrah had been described at their destruction. It was a synagogue of Satan, and it all stood before the two men in plain sight. Among the many in attendance, Abi and Tyrus did not suspect but a few to be Israelis. People had travelled from throughout the globe to see the dead bodies of the two dead men that had claimed responsibility for such disaster. The spirit of the Lord came upon both men as they were told those they looked at were doomed in their decision, referring to their taking of the mark. These were not they, whom the two were meant to save. Then, both men turned from the wicked congregation of celebrators and saw just ahead, the world media team began to assemble once more at the temple's gate, to film the third day of Deliverance, including the still-sitting in public view, bodies of Mash'pekh and Tevah.

As the two made their way to the group, both turned briefly to see the bodies of their fallen friends in the distance; the faint scent of decomposition haunting them both as they continued to walk towards the media, and in the temple public access line. At the head of the line, close to the gate, security immediately stopped both men. "Weapons check." One of the officer's said, as he grabbed Tyrus. As he did, Tevah's makeshift cane fell from Tyrus's coat. Abi walked over to the security guard that was holding Tyrus, retrieved the cane from the ground and handed it to him for inspection. My friend needs this in order to go in." he said calmly, as the security guard took the cane and looked it over. Suddenly, a scream was heard from behind Abi. The security team dropped the cane, shoved Abi to the side and saw that a drunken fight among a group of adolescences had begun, about 30 yards from where the media was covering. "Son of a…" The guard yelled as he motioned his team to break up the fight. Abi picked the cane up and handed it back to Tyrus. Tyrus looked at Abi and smiled, as the two then freely stepped into the temple entry gate and into the outside courtyard. They made their way up the pathway to the temple entrance line and saw that the line was full of people waiting to see the bodies. A heavily armored platoon of troops was guarding them; each man wearing breathing masks so not to faint from the smell of death from the two bodies that had been left mercilessly on display in the hot sun, for the full three days since they passed. As they walked along the walkway behind other visitors waiting to see Tevah and Mash'pekh, the smell of their bodies became overpowering to Abi and Tyrus. The two men did their best to hold their breath as they watched from their place in the line. As they watched people eager to spit and mock the bodies of their dead friends, three visitors, coming from the front of the line closest to the bodies, walked towards them to leave. Abi and Tyrus locked eyes with the three young women and saw that each had the mark on their foreheads. "The smell may be bad fellas, but you'll be close enough to spit on their rotting bodies!" one of them said to the two men as they walked past them, laughing wickedly. Abi and Tyrus were deeply wounded by the comment but dared not show it. They continued forward, until their place in line was right before the media's view. With the security team distracted, both men knew this was the moment they needed to step out of line and begin what they were to do. And so, the two men stepped out of the line and walked boldly towards the media.

Chapter 42

"Quiet everyone!" Ashem declared through the old microphone Jessica and her team had used to give Petra a comm system. "It's like a football stadium in here!" he declared to the massive group, as they cheered from all throughout the massive rock fortress that was to be a place of nourishment for those the Lord would soon convict. The sounds echoed throughout the caverns of the fortress, unbeknownst to the world outside. All eyes fixed on Ashem and the other leaders as they stood just before the granite rock. He cleared his throat and said, "I stood before you with a message from Tevah last night that God was about to speak to all of Israel. All of what we've done the last few years is about to take form. All our ministry and evangelism will culminate to this night. Any who watch, will be given the clearest chance to choose. Tevah told me we would be overwhelmed by what happens, but not overcome. Quite the opposite. What is about to happen, will unify the remnant of Israel and the remaining elect into an unshakeable faith that will endure for the next three and a half years." The room and adjacent caverns erupted at Ashem's words. Jessica, standing next to Ima and Maya, leaned over and while clapping for Ashem, whispered… "He's talking about the great tribulation. The last three and a half years where God punishes the wicked." Maya and Ima nodded as each clapped as well, recalling the little that Abi had shared with them about it. "Does it happen soon?" Maya asked as the crowd still cheered. Jessica nodded and leaned into her ear., saying "It's supposed to happen today. God is going to do something at the temple that will unite all the Christians that are left and turn hearts to Christ." Maya nodded. Her eyes quickly widened when she remembered Abi was still at the temple. She turned to Ima quickly. "Abi!" she exclaimed. Ima's eyes widened. "Oh, my goodness, he's there at the temple. He must be part of what's about to happen!" she declared as her mind began to entertain the worst. Jessica went over to the two, curious as to why they looked suddenly fearful. As she did, Ashem announced that the news was starting and for all to be quiet. "What is it?" Jessica asked urgently as she saw Ima crying in the back of the cavern. Maya turned towards her with tears in her eyes, and said, "My younger brother Abi is there at the temple. He was one of the two they chose to stay." Jessica's eyes widened. Her look frightened Maya. "What?" Maya asked urgently. "Jessica, what is it? What's going to happen to my little brother?" Maya asked frantically, trying her best to console Ima at the same time. The world news telecast began as Jim Massahn greeted viewers to what was expected to be a very important announcement by the Premier, from the temple. Jessica turned from Maya and looked up at the big rock where the projection was being played. "Jessica?" Maya asked, as she still tried to console Ima. Jessica turned back towards Maya and Ima with a sad look on her face, before once more looking up at the projection on the rock. As the cheers in the cavern began to hush, eager ears listened closely as the telecast went live to the foreign correspondent covering Jerusalem. The temple could be seen in the background of the broadcast by all. As each one in attendance watched and listened, they saw two figures walking towards Anne, the foreign correspondent. "Abi!" Maya screamed as she watched her brother, helplessly. Jessica ran and put her arms around Maya and Ima. "What's about to happen?" Maya whimpered, pleadingly. Jessica looked her friend and her mother in their tear-filled eyes and reluctantly replied, "You shouldn't watch this.". Maya gasped. She thought about checking for herself in Ima's Bible but knew she wouldn't find it in time to know what everyone else there seemed to already know. She looked at Jessica and Ima, helplessly as the two huddled together with her. Suddenly, Ima straightened herself up and wiped her tears from her cheeks. The small-statured woman then broke free from Maya and Jessica to both of their surprise. Ima walked past opening to where she could see the news cast for herself and watched the projection for herself. Maya wiped her tears as well and with Jessica, went to stand by Ima. Ima turned towards them both, and said, "I'm going to be with my son.". Jessica marveled at the courage of the women. The three stood together, their hands clasped as they watched Abi and Tyrus walk towards the reporters.

Chapter 43

HELLO JIM, I'M COMING to you live from the temple gates in Israel, a recurrent site for what was once hoped for as peace, but now, is the site of deliverance. We expect to hear personally from the Premier in just moments, as the rumors continue to circulate that he's now expected to set up a base of operations here at the temple and is also set to announce a new non-negotiable condition to his previous UN-backed peace agreement with Israel. We're told this drastic and necessary change was spurred forward by the events that transpired here, just three days ago. IN a statement from Darrel Denotheo, he shares "The world can no longer tolerate acts of worship, as we see here at ground zero, where we were once again witnesses to such -". Hold on Jim.... Excuse me, we're live. Excuse me, can you please back up and give us space to report? Excuse me we're live!

Abi and Tyrus approached the group of broadcasters and entered their camera view, just a few feet from where they were broadcasting, blocking out the temple from their broadcast view. Abi, wearing his cloak, stepped forward and shouted, "People of Israel and the remnant of the world! Thus says the Lord you're God!". Every eye within earshot suddenly turned towards him. "It's a zealot. Cut the feed!" Anna said, as she motioned to the camera to be turned off. She then attempted to push Abi out of frame, but as she placed her hand on his cloak, smoke emitted. She pulled her hand back to reveal it engulfed by flames. She screamed frantically, drawing the attention of even more of the raucous crowd, and especially the security detail that was still trying to break up a large fight. Anne fell to the ground, writhing in pain, as the flames on her then hand went out. She looked up at Abi and cursed at him. Abi continued into the camera. "On this day, the Lord will call every heart to him. Every heart that has not taken the mark of the beast." Tyrus stood quietly and watched as the security team began to make their way through the large group of angry onlookers, to where he and Abi stood. Abi took a step towards the camera and gazed into it as if making a final appeal from the Lord. The furious screams of the security team grew louder as they made their way closer to them. Abi exhaled and spoke… "Today, you will know the God of Abraham, the God of Isaac and the God of Jacob is the God of our Lord Jesus Christ. Today, as the world celebrates its deliverance from God, God responds with His final appeal. Those of you who hear his voice will be told by the spirit where to go and you will believe it with conviction. The rest of the world will now incur the full wrath of God!" Abi then became overwhelmed by the spirit and began repeating that last sentence in other foreign languages, to the shock of those who were there, seeing it. As he was speaking, the security team suddenly rushed in front of Abi and Tyrus. But as they reached for the two, Tyrus drew out Tevah's cane and through it to the ground before them. The cane turned immediately into a large and deadly serpent. It uncoiled itself and attempted to violently strike the men, who were terrified. They and the reporters, all fled into the crowd, leaving behind their many cameras that were still capturing the live feed. As the screams of the reporters and security detail were heard from deep within the crowd, the onlookers became enraged and soon began to pour inside the temple gate, as their wicked numbers continued to grow. "Kill them!" some of them shouted, as the crowd looked for a way to move past the serpent that guarded the two. As the revelers inched closer and closer to Abi and Tyrus; all bearing the Premier's mark, Abi continued unimpeded, speaking by the spirit in different languages to the camera. The crowd, still unable to get past the serpent, gnashed their teeth at the two men, when suddenly a massive eruption from the sky was heard. All who were there, looked up to see the sky seemingly ripped open, as light then beamed brightly down to the bodies of Mash'pekh and Tevah. The crowd screamed and bellowed out in their fear, but none could move or look away. Then, all who were there were made immediately silent in their terror, as a loud and thunderous voice overwhelmed the entire world, as it called out from the sky... "Thus says the Lord, rise, Moses." The voice said as Tevah's body suddenly rose and was once more made whole. Tevah's eyes opened with flames. Those who watched from home and around the world fell to their knees at the sight. Then, the same thunderous voice called out... "Thus says the Lord, rise, Elijah.", as the once-broken body of Mash'pekh was then instantly restored. The two prophets gloriously stood in the presence of all the world; those in attendance and the many eyes that watched the broadcast. Ashem, watching with the colony in Petra, stood dumfounded, as none of the men who had been gathered together, knew of the men's true identities. Ashem looked around at the men, who each stood in awe, praising the God of Israel, and said, "They came to their own and their own did not recognize them. Just as it was with Christ." he declared as those around him and throughout gave praise to God, in the name of Jesus.

Chapter 44

As the prophets stood, shining in Heaven's glory for all to see; their mortal wounds completely healed, the thunderous voice from Heaven called out again… "Come up here.". The two men, beaming brilliantly, lifted off the ground, with their hands held towards Heaven. Abi and Tyrus watched as the men they knew were taken from their sight, in the clouds. The opening in the sky then closed, as thunder began to erupt, and lightning flashed. Tyrus bent down and grabbed the serpent, who at once returned to a cane. The crowd, still standing without movement, surrounding the two men, watched as Tyrus stepped forward; their eyes fixed on the young man's cane. Tyrus looked at the crowd, before looking to Heaven, saying "It is just!". He then took the butt of his cane and struck the ground before him, seven times. Suddenly, a rumble in the sky occurred. Abi watched as a powerful angel from heaven descended from the clouds onto the ground before them. The onlookers couldn't see him, only those who had been convicted of what they saw, could see the angel in his terrifying glory. The angel sneered at the wicked group that surrounded the temple. He then struck the ground with his fist and suddenly the entire nation of Israel shook, violently. An unmeasurable earthquake erupted, incomparable in its power. The earthquake was so great, it ripped itself across the entire Middle East and caused destruction to all nations throughout, opening thousands and thousands of large random holes in the ground, the likes of what Abi and Tyrus had witnessed in their dreams. Then, as the earthquakes rumbles their utter destruction throughout, the live feed at the temple was suddenly cut off. Maya and Ima gasped, as the world around Petra, seemed to shake violently. The angel that descended, turned towards Abi and Cyrus, and nodded, before returning to the skies of Heaven. The two men watched as those in attendance, the bearers of the beast's mark, were destroyed by the great earthquake. Buildings erupted before them, falling on helpless onlookers. The ground opened itself up to swallow those who had been just celebrating a few moments earlier. None were spared as suddenly; the inner city itself was swallowed up in billowing smoke.

As those in Petra watched the feed of news die, their hearts began to sink. Siff looked at Danny and marveled. "The whole time, it was HIM!" He said overwhelmed at the thought of Moses being among them. Jessica stood next to her team, dumfounded by the revelation as each just stared towards each other, marveling. Maya turned towards Ima and was too grieved to marvel. "I'm sure he got out of there." She whispered to her mother. Ima looked up towards the rock that was used as a screen, desperate for any indication of what happened to her son. Jessica moved from her team to check on Maya and Ima, as both women were hugging each other through sobs. Maya turned towards Jessica and scowled. "Did you know?" she asked, coldly. Jessica nodded. "I knew there was going to be an earthquake, yes. It's in the Bible. I didn't know anything but that." She said, assuredly. Maya shook her head and turned from her. Jessica watched as Maya again focused on a smaller picture than the one Jessica was forced to realize. She felt herself overcome with truth and scolded Maya, saying, "Each of us answered a call, Maya. God chose Abi. God chose Abi out of all these people to do what we all just saw. Don't you see that? Don't you see what an honor that is? The Prophet Isaiah was sawn in two. The Apostles all died horrible deaths. Jesus died the most painful death we could imagine. But greater is our reward in heaven, Maya!" Maya turned towards Jessica and saw tears streaming down her face. She then felt Ima uncouple herself from her hug. Ima wiped her face of her tears and walked over to Jessica. She looked into Jessica's blue eyes that were now filled with an expression both she and maya had never seen…. Ima knew the pain Jessica was carrying. "You've lost more than soldiers, haven't you?" Ima asked her. Jessica, her eyes overwhelmed with tears, nodded quietly. "I lost my mom and sister." Jessica admitted, as she wiped her face. Ima hugged her tightly. "Does it ever get easier?" Ima asked as she pulled back and wiped a flurry of tears from Jessica's face. Jessica shook her head, before saying "It doesn't. It will never be easy to lose people. I think that's why Jesus wept. Not because He didn't understand death or thought it was final, but because of what the pain from loss does to our soul. It doesn't get easier, no. But those who are saved, like your son and my mother and my sister, wait for us where Jesus wipes our tears away." Ima melted into Jessica's arms as the two embraced once more. Maya watched as Jessica and Ima hugged each other free of tears, knowing the burdens each had quietly carried. Jessica never let on about the family she lost. Jessica wasn't an open person. But Maya understood why she had seemingly taken such a liking to her and Ima. Though her rugged exterior and bravado held such camouflage to the pain she had personally undertaken, Maya and Ima were a sense of normalization for Jessica. A return to the family she once had and loved. Maya knew in that moment why she and Jessica had bonded so quickly. She knew she would need to lean on Jessica as a sister, now. She made her way over to the two women and joined them in their embrace, finding peace in the Lord's will.

Chapter 45

ASHEM AWOKE THAT MORNING and rose to his feet. He went out to the main area, where they had continued to watch for news. No live feed had been given since the earthquake. Though two days had passed, there was no news to be heard. Ashem motioned to Mike, who was standing at the catacomb where the projection was running. "Was there anything at all during the night?" Mike shook his head. Ashem looked somber. "Patience. They'll come!" he assured himself as he made his way through one of the tunnels to the ration room, for breakfast. As he entered, he saw Maya just sitting down. He grabbed a ration box and made his way over to her. "Can I sit with you?" he asked. Maya smiled and nodded. Ashem sat down, as the two began to eat. "Your brother was quite an individual." He said to Maya as her eyes stayed fixed on her food. Maya swallowed the spoonful of meat she had grown accustomed to and looked over to him. "Did you know him?" she asked. Ashem smiled and replied, "I knew of him." Maya looked puzzled. "What do you mean?" She asked. Ashem put his fork down and turned toward her, and said, "When I first met Moses... sorry, Tevah, he told me that I would not receive his powers when he was gone. I didn't understand it at the time, and it brought me a lot of bitterness. As I understand it now though, I see it better. Your brother and Tyrus were both very special people. They were the only ones in Israel who would have enough blind faith to receive the Lord's power and use it for His purpose, will and glory. That's no ordinary calling." Ashem said, as he smiled at the thought, before turning back to his food. Maya nodded at the thought as she continued to eat her meal. "I guess I don't see the significance." She replied, as she put another fork full of the gelatin-based meat in her mouth. Ashem turned again to her and smiled. "Maya, only two men in the Bible have ever done what your brother and Tyrus were called to do. Maya paused mid-bite, before putting her fork down and turning towards Ashem. She squinted as she thought what he was implying. Then a thought came to her.... "Moses and Elijah?" she asked. Ashem shook his head in response and chuckled. "No, not the men God bestowed the power to. Not them. Their greatness was God-chosen, and both saw things that made them believe in the power they were given." Maya frowned. She didn't understand. Ashem leaned into her and whispered… "What about the men who followed those men, who were then asked to take their powers and walk as they did? Who among us would walk so humbly and faithfully in *their* footsteps, being suddenly given God's power or wisdom? Which is the harder calling, after all? Receiving the power after hearing the voice of God, or receiving that power from someone who says they heard the voice of God? No, give me the faith of Elisha and Joshua in those moments. They didn't need to see to believe. They each believed and never looked back. That is exactly what we saw in Abi and Tyrus. Conviction to win a holy war, mixed with humility. None of us could do what they did. And I speak from a place of great disappointment in myself over that.", Ashem said, as he smiled and returned to his food, taking a large bite of the canned meat. Maya marveled at the thought and pondered over what Ashem said. She understood the qualities he was referring to when she thought of her brother. She smiled proudly as she lifted her ration box from the stone they were sitting at together. "Thanks for those beautiful words, Ash Ash!" she said playfully, smiling towards Ashem as she left. Ashem smiled and whispered to himself, "I like that nickname…", before eagerly returning to what remained of his food. As he enjoyed thought, the compound alarm sounded.

Chapter 46

THE ALARM SWEPT THROUGH the tunnels of Petra, as Siff's voice was heard on the intercom. "Attention, Jessica, Ashem, Tomas, we have inbound." Ashem got up from the table and ran to the front entry point of the rock. He saw Tomas there, holding binoculars. "Well?" Ashem asked, as he impatiently waited for an update from Tomas. "It could be the start. But it could be OWL. I'm not sure until they get closer." Tomas said, as he continued to watch. Ashem turned and made his way down the rocky stairs. "We're not expecting OWL today!" he declared faithfully. He leapt from the bottom stair and made his way to the great stone room, to find Jessica. "Who is it?" she asked Ashem as she and her team were in the process of loading their weapons, quickly. "I'm not sure yet, but I don't think we'll be needing those to say the least." Ashem responded loudly, his voice growing loud as he rebuked the thought of any protection but the Lord's. Jessica did not challenge him. She looked over to Justin and said, "Stow them.", which was her orders to hide the weapons. Justin nodded as he, Mike, Tyrell, and Amy rounded up the guns and ammunition, before placing them in their team's cave.

Jessica ran to catch up with Ashem who was standing at the entry tunnel, as Maya and Ima joined as well. Crowds of the men inside the fortress began to form at the large basin, near the opening. The men stood eager to hear what was happening, as Ashem called their leaders up to where he was standing. They all watched as thick pillars of dust began to rise from out in the desert, due to the many vehicles that were now headed towards them. Just then, the first of the many vehicles came fully into view. "It is them!" Tomas declared, as he watched the many different vehicles skirting across the desert plain through the dried-out trench they too, had traveled through. Many of the families that the 144,000 had ministered to over the weeks, months, and years of their march, were now making their way across the dry desert, and speeding towards Petra, just as Tevah said they would. The group rejoiced. "Ima!" Tomas yelled out from where he was watching. Ima perked up at the call of her name. She looked up from where she was standing, towards Ashem. Ashem smiled towards her and Maya. "They're being led by your son." Ashem said stoically, as the entire cavern erupted at the news that Abi and Tyrus were not only alive but leading the first group of Israelis to safety. Ima burst into tears as she and Maya rejoiced at the news. Then, Tomas shrieked out.... "It's OWL!" Ashem turned and looked through the binoculars, seeing that just a few yards behind the band of vehicles headed for Petra, was a massive battalion of OWL soldiers; their vehicles just coming over the ridge of the first dune. "Oh my gosh, please no." Ima said, her voice shrieking from within the cave. They watched nervously as the band of Israeli's moved to within a few yards of the entry point, when suddenly, the leading car being driven by Tyrus and Abi, suddenly turned off. None of the other vehicles followed him, as the fleeing Israelis made their way to Petra, and were immediately met, as they were aided into the fortress.

Chapter 47

THE MEN OF THE 144,000, having ran to their aid, helped to carry the sick, elderly and lame in through the rocky structures until all were inside. All but Abi and Tyrus, who were now driving into the storm of OWL vehicles, barreling towards them. "What are they doing?" Maya screamed as she helplessly watched. Then, the truck containing Abi and Tyrus came to an immediate stop in the middle of the same basin where Jessica and the team had met up with Ashem, when each first arrived. Everyone inside of Petra watched as the two men stepped out of the vehicle to face the horde of OWL soldiers. Ima and Maya embraced one another as their beloved Abi stepped in front of his truck, quickly followed by Tyrus. Abi placed Mash'pekh's cloak down, while Tyrus placed Tevah's cane on top of it. They then backed away several feet before both falling to their knees and praying, as OWL's forces accelerated into the basin, they were in. The two then called out... "Lord we give thanks for the gift of your power. Protect this remnant and the remnants still to come. Give us our protector and unleash them!" As they prayed, the united remnant of Israel watched the entire sky instantly illuminate. Suddenly, an opening through the clouds appeared just as the one that Tevah and Mash'pekh had ascended through. And out from the opening, descended a large and powerful angel. He flew to the ground just before Abi and Tyrus, where they had laid their cloak and cane. The ground shook as he landed in the sand. His glory was indescribable, as he beamed his heavenly light across the desert, unbeknownst to OWL. The angel watched as the forces of OWL moved closer, unable to see him. He raised his hand towards Heaven and cried out… "Lord your servant, the protector of Israel and leader of your armies swears that it shall be done. All shall be done. I Michael, the protector of Israel, declare it in your name, Lord!" He spoke aloud, his voice thundering throughout all of Petra. The remnant stood awestruck at the sight of Michael, standing before them in the Lord's glory. As the Archangel pronounced his oath, in the distance, a great tremble came over the desert and surrounding areas, as a large crack, similar to the ones emerging from the great earthquake, began to suddenly form between Michael and the OWL platoon. The vehicles came to an immediate stop at the gaping hole. The platoon of OWL soldiers each stepped out of their vehicles to investigate the gaping hole as it increased in size. Then, Michael called out with a thunderous cry… "Abaddon… release them!". Then, from the depths of the hole and the other holes that had formed across the globe from the earthquake, smoke began to pour outward. The Earth then erupted forward, through the smoke, millions upon millions of the horrifying and demonic looking insect-like beings that Abi and Tyrus had both witnessed in their dreams. The skies filled as they burst forward throughout the world, into every country and every city. Abi and Tyrus, watched as their questions of "who are they?" were immediately answered. The prophesied locusts, with their sharp, venomous tails, attacked the forces of OWL, stinging them without mercy, amidst their cries and pleas. Michael shouted in the air once more and the now millions of locusts lifted away from the fallen OWL platoon, who were lying paralyzed by their sting. As the locusts flew towards Petra, those who watched, began to scream in fear as the swarm barreled towards their direction. "Peace be still! You are sealed! They will not harm you!" Ashem cried out to the leaders as each echoed out his words to the crowd. Then, the ominous locust swarm flew over Petra, to join the rest of their numbers throughout the world, in tormenting anyone who wasn't sealed by God. Michael, seeing the OWL soldiers scattered on the ground, still writhing in their agony, raised himself into the air and looked up to heaven… "It is just!" he shouted, as he then looked down at those who were paralyzed by the stings of the locusts. He then called fire from Heaven, down on the paralyzed forces, incinerating them and their equipment, instantly. Michael saw no souls remaining. He then turned towards Petra and beheld the first remnant that was redeemed, standing alongside the 144,000. It was a joyous sight to his eyes; one long-awaited. He had long watched them and knew that they had been delivered out of the time of Jacob's sorrow that was coming. "Glory and praise be to you, Lord." He said proudly as he then lifted swiftly into the sky, returned to Heaven. Abi, amazed by what he saw, looked out where Michael was standing, and saw the staff and cloak were gone. He looked over and smiled at Tyrus. Both men then returned to their truck and made their way to the fortress, as they joined the others at Petra; the place prepared in the wilderness for those who stood

Chapter 48

THIS IS A WORLD *News Special… Good evening, everyone this is Jim Massahn here with breaking news. Just a reminder… stay tuned afterwards for our coverage of the United Scientific Panel that will be discussing the fascinating star anomaly Mr. Denotheo and team are calling, "Wormwood". But for now, we go live to the former Jerusalem temple, where just over a month ago, we tragically lost our very own Anne Frederick, who was one of seven thousand to be killed in the massive earthquake that shook the middle east – most of which was caught on film. We are told the Premier will now be giving his long-awaited press conference as to the changes he is instituting on behalf of the former and now disbanded United Nations. We go live now…*

Just two months ago, I stood before the world and gave it the power to defend itself. This, the same place where my own life was nearly taken. I proved beyond a doubt, that religion was the weapon chosen to divide us and destroy us. The evidence was so convincing, that the United Nations elected me as their leader. A single voice, crying out from the wilderness – religion was given to destroy us. You all cheered this message. You all saw evidence. You all agreed. And, just a few days later, the extra-terrestrials responsible for the disappearing, used simple holographic projections to deceive Israel and the world over, that the religion that was meant to enslave us, should still humorously be embraced! They tested our intelligence and understanding, vs our old ways of thinking. They tested our resolve and commitment to abolishing any weapon they use against us. We, as a people, failed their test. We failed it because no matter what we prove or what we show you, those of you who hold to the dangers of baseless and debunked faith, will always be a threat to the enlightened society around you. So, I announce, having been given the full authority of the recently disbanded United Nations and the full authority of the 10 leaders of the green summit, that our world changes, today. What once was just a suggestion, or an urging will now become life or death, for any person caught in the act of belief, expressing faith, or being implicated as such. The punishment will be the same as it is for anyone who refused link18. Your head will be removed from your body. Your choices and refusal to comply will no longer be a danger to the rest of our society. As such, I have revoked Israel's right to worship in this temple or anywhere else, effective immediately. Given the civil unrest of Israel and their repeated violations of the agreement, I will now assume full control of this temple and will commandeer it as a peacekeeping throne, where I promise to move us forward, despite our failures. Those who fled after the events that transpired here, will be hunted, and eliminated as we now understand they assisted the foreign invaders in this great deception. That is correct. We have learned in the last few weeks that those who refer to themselves as the remnant of Israel, were involved in both the disappearing and the deception. They continue to believe that the foreign invaders are their Gods and prophets. Enough! To them I say, we will hunt you down and we will eliminate the threat of your existence.

To the nearly three billion faithful inhabitants of this glorious planet, we call Mother Earth, I thank you for your continued loyalty, your bravery against such horror and you're courage to be heard. I challenge you, our faithful, to join us in turning over every stone and piece of debris necessary, until the threat of every "link less" man and woman is neutralized. If they haven't received the gift of link18 yet, it is now safe to assume they are no longer on our side, or even human. And, as such, they should not be treated as anything but an extreme danger to our society. Remember, this is a war. I set out as your leader to win. They've poisoned our lands. They've poisoned our waters. They've unleashed their experiments in our atmosphere, resulting in every catastrophe you have seen and been struck by. Their locusts and hail, fire, and brimstone, all that they've done.... There is no defense for any person who aids them. We must unite for the good of our society. Do not believe their lies. Houses will be divided. This is the price our society now pays for religion and the infestation it causes. So, to those who think they won't be caught, to those who feel their "god" will protect them or to those who put their own selfishness over the needs of society, please know, you won't be privy to society much longer. You can no longer buy a thing. You can no longer eat a thing. You can no longer talk to anyone. We know who you are. Every person with link18 has in their database, your identification and picture. You will be seen; you will be caught, and you will be beheaded. Society is now linked as one. Linked to me. We are one.

I will find every single one of you Christians, and I will destroy you. I am coming.

If you can't remember the date
If you can't remember the time
If you can't remember the moment
Stop everything and say these words...

Jesus, I believe YOU are the Son of God,
that YOU died on the cross to rescue me
from sin and death and to restore me to the
Father. I choose now to turn from my sins,
my self-centeredness, and every part of my
life that does not please YOU. I choose
YOU. I give myself to YOU

Don't ASSUME your salvation

ASSURE it!

About the Author

MATTHEW J. FRATUS IS an author and artist, in North Carolina. He is the founder of Zeal Artistry, a ministerial effort creating Christian-themed artwork for the sole purpose of philanthropy. Matthew's poetry and artwork have been both acclaimed critically and published nationally. Matthew married his loving wife, Brittany, in 2004. They have been blessed with two wonderful children (Matthew and Cali).